JUST A MEMORY AWAY

In hospital, Alison Montgomery cannot remember her own name. She hears the doctors' hushed whispers — sees their worried glances, which speak of the dark secrets lying just beyond the locked shutters of her memory. Then they bring her the stranger who says he's her husband. But why can't she remember loving a man as compelling as Nicholas Montgomery? And yet the shadows in his eyes clearly reveal that there's something in their past better left forgotten . . .

MOYRA TARLING

JUST A MEMORY AWAY

Complete and Unabridged

LINFORD
Leicester

First published in The United States of America
in 1993

First Linford Edition
published 2012

All the characters in this book have no existence
outside the imagination of the author and have
no relation whatsoever to anyone bearing the
same name or names. They are not even distantly
inspired by any individual known or unknown to
the author, and all incidents are pure invention.

British Library CIP Data

Tarling, Moyra.
    Just a memory away.- -
    (Linford romance library)
    1. Love stories.
    2. Large type books.
    I. Title II. Series
    823.9′2–dc23

    ISBN 978–1–4448–1075–2

Published by
F. A. Thorpe (Publishing)
Anstey, Leicestershire

Set by Words & Graphics Ltd.
Anstey, Leicestershire
Printed and bound in Great Britain by
T. J. International Ltd., Padstow, Cornwall

This book is printed on acid-free paper

To Leanne, my daughter,
my friend.
You've only just begun.
GO FOR IT!

1

The young woman lying on the hospital bed stirred briefly before her eyes fluttered open. Pain, sharp and unexpected, throbbed somewhere inside her skull and she moaned softly in protest.

At the sound, the nurse who'd been seated in a chair nearby stood up and approached the bed. 'It's all right, Mrs. Montgomery. Just lie still,' she said in a reassuring tone.

'What happened? Where am I?'

'Bayview Hospital,' came the prompt reply.

'Bayview?' She repeated the name with a frown. 'I don't understand.' She tried to sit up.

'Take it easy, you don't want to dislodge your intravenous.' The nurse's voice was calm and soothing.

'I can't seem to remember . . . ' Her voice trailed off and she closed her eyes as the pain inside her head intensified. She took several deep breaths, waiting for it to subside. Bayview Hospital — that was what the nurse had said, but the name didn't mean a thing.

'You had us all worried, Mrs. Montgomery,' she heard the nurse say, and felt cool fingers at her wrist. 'Especially your husband.'

Her eyes flew open and she felt her pulse quicken. 'My husband?' The words came out in a throaty whisper.

The nurse nodded and smiled. 'He'll be so relieved to know you're awake. Do you know that for the past two nights he's slept right there on that chair?' She nodded toward the chair she'd only vacated moments ago. 'I'd better stop chattering and go and find him,' she said as she patted her patient's pillows. 'You'll be anxious to see him, too.' She smiled once more, then turned and headed toward the door.

My name isn't Mrs. Montgomery! The words screamed inside her head as the door silently closed behind the nurse. She felt her pulse gather speed as feelings of fear and confusion sprang to life within her.

The nurse had made a mistake, that was all, she told herself calmly, trying without success to ignore her racing heart. When the nurse returned she would simply explain that there'd been some kind of mix-up . . . that she wasn't Mrs. Montgomery, that her name was — Her thoughts came to a jarring halt.

'My name is . . . ' She spoke the words aloud in the hope that her brain would simply fill in the blank. But to her astonishment she couldn't seem to remember anything.

Who am I? The question echoed inside her head and suddenly she found it difficult to breathe as she groped frantically for her identity. It was utterly ridiculous not to know her own name, she kept telling herself. But the harder she tried to concentrate on who she was, the more unbearable the pain in her head became.

Her fingers clutched convulsively at the bedcovers as she fought to control the panic threatening to overwhelm her.

Closing her eyes, she forced herself to take one deep breath, then another. She was having a nightmare. That was it! And any minute now she'd wake up. Tentatively, she opened her eyes, but nothing had changed.

Dismay had her trembling like a leaf. This couldn't be happening! She lowered her gaze to stare down at her hands gripping the sheet, her knuckles white with tension. Her glance flickered from the intravenous drip to the shiny gold band on the fourth finger of her left hand. Before she could think or react to its presence, the door swung open and she found herself staring at the most stunningly attractive man she'd ever seen.

That he was a doctor was obvious by the white hospital coat he wore, a coat that served to accentuate his dark good looks. Hair as black as coal was swept back from a face that could only be described as mesmerizing. Dark fathomless eyes held hers for what seemed an eternity and she felt a shiver of awareness dance across her skin.

A flicker of emotion flashed briefly in his eyes and a look of expectation appeared on his handsome features. He seemed to be waiting for her to say something, but she could only stare in bewildered silence as feelings of anxiety and confusion held her firmly in their grasp.

'You *are* awake.' His voice was deep and sensuous and infinitely disturbing.

She could only nod in response, an action that brought with it a fresh wave of pain, making her grimace.

In an instant he was at her side, a look of concern evident in the dark depths of his eyes. 'Headache? And a bad one, too, right?' he said softly, but before she could respond, he continued. 'It would be a miracle if you didn't have a headache, after what happened.' He paused to study her intently for a long moment. 'Tell me. What on earth were you doing out in the middle of the street?' he asked, and there was no mistaking the underlying anger in his words.

She had no idea what he was talking about, but strangely she wished she could somehow give him the explanation he seemed to need.

'I'm sorry,' she mumbled, and dropped her gaze, fighting to hold back the tears suddenly threatening to overwhelm her.

'You gave us all quite a scare,' she heard him say and then felt his hand close around her wrist, his fingers deftly locating her pulse point.

At his touch, her breath caught in her throat and she had the weirdest sensation that she was sinking, almost as if she'd stepped into quicksand and slowly but steadily she was being dragged under.

'I'm sorry,' she said again, her voice wavering with emotion. The pounding in her head was beginning to make her feel nauseous, and not for the first time, she wondered if this was just a bad dream.

When her glance came to rest once more on the gold wedding band on her left hand, a fresh wave of panic roiled up inside her. A zillion questions began to buzz inside her head like bees trapped in a jar. But before she could voice the one question burning a hole in her brain, he spoke again.

'I'll speak to the nurse about getting a painkiller for you,' he said. 'That should get you over the worst.'

'Thank you,' she managed. 'Ah . . . could you tell me — ' She stopped suddenly, confused and not a little embarrassed.

'Tell you what?' His tone was gentle.

She felt her eyes fill with tears at the tenderness in his voice. 'I'm sorry . . . ' she began. 'It's just that I can't seem to remember — ' She broke off, feeling foolish.

'You mean, you don't remember the accident?'

'Accident?' she repeated with a

frown. 'No, I don't remember the accident,' she replied, relieved that he didn't appear perturbed by the revelation.

'Don't worry. Under the circumstances, that's perfectly normal,' he quietly assured her.

Slowly she shook her head. 'No . . . you don't understand,' she went on. 'The nurse said she was going to find my husband . . . '

'Yes,' he said with a puzzled smile.

'You don't understand,' she repeated earnestly, her agitation growing. 'I don't *have* a husband . . . at least, if I do, I don't remember. Oh God . . . nothing makes any sense.' Tears filled her eyes and she tried to blink them away as she lifted her gaze to meet his. 'I don't remember anything. I don't know who I am . . . I don't even know my own name.'

Her words this time were met with total silence. The look of surprise that flashed briefly in the depths of his dark eyes gave way to another emotion, one

8

she couldn't so easily define. The air between them crackled with tension and she found the silence somehow threatening. The tears she'd been trying hard to control, overflowed.

'Hey . . . don't cry,' he soothed gently, putting his hand over hers in a gesture of comfort. 'You have every right to be upset. But, please, try not to worry. Amnesia after an accident or a crack on the head like the one you received, isn't uncommon and in most cases it lasts a few hours or at the most a few days. Your memory will come back.' His tone reassured her. 'You just have to give it time.' He reached for the box of tissues on the table by the bed and handed it to her.

'Thanks,' she mumbled, and managed a weak smile as she pulled several tissues free and blew her nose.

She lay back against the pillows and sighed, unsure why she should feel comforted by the fact that this doctor seemed certain her memory would return. But silently she acknowledged that there was something about this man, an unmistakable confidence and an air of quiet authority, that was impossible to ignore.

'The nurse called me Mrs. Montgomery,' she said after a moment. 'Is that really my name?' she asked.

'Yes,' he answered after the briefest of hesitations. 'Alison Montgomery.'

'Alison?' she repeated, and at his nod she closed her eyes. 'Alison Montgomery.' She spoke the name aloud, hoping that by doing so she might unlock the door to her memory, but instead the pain inside her head seemed to take on a new dimension and she groaned and lifted her hands to massage her throbbing temples.

'Don't force it.' The low rumble of his voice cut through her empty thoughts.

'Nothing. I don't remember anything!' Frustration and annoyance brought fresh tears to her eyes. 'My mind is completely and utterly blank, like a slate wiped clean.' She went on, a catch in her voice. 'I don't know who I am, or where I am . . . '

'Don't . . . you're only upsetting yourself,' he told her gently. 'Your memory will return, you have to believe that. But first things first. You need something for that headache.'

Alison fought to maintain control, hating herself for feeling weak and dependent. 'I just wish I didn't feel so lost,' she said.

'Everything will be all right.' He followed his words with a reassuring smile before turning and heading to the door.

'Doctor?'

'Yes?' He stopped in the open doorway.

'I was wondering . . . ah . . . the nurse said she was going to find my . . . my husband.' She tripped over the word that sounded so foreign to her ears. 'I'm not sure . . . I mean . . . I don't quite know . . . ' She faltered and looked away, feeling her face grow hot with embarrassment. But suddenly the thought of having to deal with another stranger, even though he was her husband, was more than she was ready to face.

'I'll take care of it,' he cut in, and there was no mistaking the edge in his voice.

Sensitive to the change in his tone, Alison glanced up, immediately noticing a tension in his features that hadn't been there before. He held her gaze for a long moment and not for the first time since he'd walked into the room, she had the distinct impression he was waiting for something.

'Thank you,' she said, but the door was already closing and she frowned, puzzled by his reaction.

Alison leaned back, feeling drained and very tired. The pain in her head had eased fractionally, and though she wasn't someone who used aspirin very often, right now she would welcome the relief they would bring.

She gasped, realizing that her thoughts had just revealed a small personal detail about herself. Small and insignificant though the information might be, she had to believe it was a beginning.

She smiled, her spirits lifting several notches. Reaching up, she ran her hand through her hair and winced as her fingers came in contact with a sizable swelling just below the crown of her head. Probing gently, she discovered that a dressing had been applied to the area.

The doctor had said she'd been in an accident. Hadn't he asked her what she'd been doing in the street? Perhaps she'd been in a car accident? Closing her eyes, Alison drew a deep breath and tried to remember.

Nothing. What had she been doing? Where had she been going? With a weary sigh, she opened her eyes and began to twist a strand of her hair around her finger, realizing as she did that her hair was shoulder-length and inclined to curl.

Suddenly the thought struck her that

she didn't even know what she looked like. Pulling a handful of hair forward, she noted that it was a rich chocolate brown in color, but a quick glance around the hospital room revealed no sign of a mirror.

What did she look like? What color were her eyes? How old was she? Did she have a job? Did she and her husband have any children? What about her family? Mother, father, sisters, brothers? The questions came fast and furious, as if she'd opened a floodgate, but as each question remained unanswered feelings of panic began to resurface.

She had to force herself to stay calm and she tried not to think about just how she was going to deal with this emptiness.

The nurse had only spoken of her husband and all at once there settled over her a strong conviction that she had no family, that she was alone in the world, except for her husband.

Her thoughts somehow always seemed

to come back to him. What was he like? Did she love him? Of course she must love him — she'd married him. How she wished she could remember.

Hadn't the nurse said something about her husband sleeping in the chair for the past two nights? Had she really been unconscious for that length of time? Where was her husband now? What was his name?

While part of her wanted to see him, thinking that perhaps when she did her memory would come rushing back, another part of her was filled with apprehension.

How she hated feeling helpless and out of control. The questions continued to bombard her and when she heard the door to her room open anxiety rippled through her as she glanced up at her visitor.

Relief washed over her and she felt her heart skip a beat at the sight of the handsome, dark-haired doctor. It seemed strange to her that after what had only been a brief exchange earlier she should already consider him a friend, but she did. She smiled a welcome, but her smile wavered a little when she noticed he wasn't alone.

Behind him came an older gray-haired man, also wearing a white hospital coat.

'Alison, I'd like you to meet Dr. Jacobson. He's the hospital's psychologist.'

'Dr. Jacobson,' Alison said.

'Hello, Alison,' the older man acknowledged. 'I'm glad to see you looking so well.' His blue eyes regarded her kindly. 'Nick has just been telling me that you're having a problem with your memory. Is that right?'

Alison nodded, throwing a glance at the man Dr. Jacobson had called Nick. His gaze met hers unwaveringly and for a fleeting second something flashed inside her head — a memory? She couldn't be sure — but before she could grasp it and hold on, it was gone.

'Tell me, what do you remember?' Dr. Jacobson asked, breaking into her reverie.

Alison frowned as she brought her attention back to the older man. 'Absolutely nothing,' she replied. 'When I woke up I had no idea who or where I was . . . ' Her voice faltered as the fear and confusion returned.

'It's all right,' Dr. Jacobson said calmly. 'Believe me, it's not uncommon. The first thing you need to know is that there is no reason to believe your memory loss is permanent. But on the other hand, it's impossible to predict exactly when or how it will return.

'Interaction with people, places and even certain smells and sights often act as a trigger mechanism, bringing back incidents and moments from your past, until bit by bit the empty spaces inside your mind will all be filled up.'

'But wouldn't it be easier if you simply told me about my past, about who I am and what I do?' Alison asked, impatience edging her voice.

Dr. Jacobson took her hand in his and smiled. 'I understand how you must feel, believe me. And there are some things you will certainly have to be told.' He stopped and glanced at Nick before continuing. 'But in your case, I feel that the best course of action is to take things a step at a time. It's quite possible you'll go to sleep tonight and wake up in the morning remembering everything,' he ended on an encouraging note.

'Does that mean you aren't going to tell me anything about myself? That I'm supposed to wait until my memory returns on its own?' Her voice rose slightly in agitation.

'That's my recommendation, yes,' Dr. Jacobson said, and smiled reassuringly at her. 'Alison, trust me, your feelings of anxiety and fear *will* pass.'

She held his gaze, wanting to believe him. Suddenly a thought struck her. 'Have you discussed this with my husband? Does he agree? Maybe it's time I saw him . . . you said yourself it might trigger something.' Alison tried with difficulty to quell the feelings of anxiety swamping her.

But Dr. Jacobson's advice that she remain in the dark brought the panic rushing back. She wished she'd had the courage earlier to see her husband. Why hadn't they insisted he be present? Perhaps he'd gone home to rest? But surely he had a right to know what was going on?

'I want to see my husband.' She spoke abruptly and at her words Dr. Jacobson seemed genuinely taken aback. He glanced at Nick and again Alison noted the swift but silent exchange between the two men.

'What's wrong?' she asked apprehensively. 'You said you'd talk to him and tell him about my loss of memory.' She was staring now at Nick, who'd been quiet throughout the other doctor's speech.

'Be assured, he knows everything about your condition,' Nick said easily, but Alison couldn't shake the feeling that there was something he wasn't telling her.

'Nick,' Dr. Jacobson cautioned. 'I

think it's time you told her.'

'Told me what?' Alison asked, trying to calm the butterflies fluttering in her stomach.

Nick approached the bed and took her hand in his and at the contact Alison felt her pulse accelerate in alarm. His dark eyes held hers for a breathless moment before he spoke.

'I was hoping you'd remember on your own,' he said softly.

'Remember what?' Alison held his gaze, suddenly feeling as if she was standing on the edge of a cliff, fearful that what he was about to tell her would send her toppling over the edge.

'My name is Nicholas Montgomery,' he told her in a calm voice. 'I am your husband.'

2

Alison stared in openmouthed astonishment at the man who claimed to be her husband. It couldn't be true! Surely she would remember if she was married to someone as devastatingly attractive as Nicholas Montgomery.

'You don't remember?' The question came from Dr. Jacobson and Alison had to drag her eyes away from Nick's.

She swallowed and shook her head. 'No, I don't remember.' She was beginning to sound like a broken record.

Dr. Jacobson smiled encouragingly. 'Don't upset yourself. Try not to worry.'

At the concern in the older man's voice, Alison felt the tears well up in her eyes, and she dropped her gaze, noting with some surprise that she was gripping Nick's hand as though she might never let go.

'Oh . . . sorry,' she mumbled, and

released her hold on him, suddenly feeling awkward and embarrassed. She heard Nick's sigh, undoubtedly of exasperation, and closed her eyes, wishing fervently that none of this was happening.

It had been traumatic enough waking up and realizing that she had no memory of the past, but learning that she was married . . .

Someone rapped softly on the hospital room door and Alison opened her eyes in time to see the nurse who'd attended her earlier enter the room. In her hands was a tray with a glass of water and a tiny paper cup.

'Excuse me, Doctor,' the nurse said. 'I've brought the medication for Mrs. Montgomery.'

'Thank you, Nurse Lucas,' Nick replied, moving to take the tray from her hands.

Turning, he set the tray on the table at the foot of the bed and rolled the table toward Alison. 'For your headache,' he said, offering her the tiny cup, which contained two pills.

Alison accepted the pills and after swallowing them lay back against the pillows.

'You look tired, my dear,' Dr. Jacobson commented. 'This has been rather traumatic for you. We'll leave you to rest awhile.'

'I *am* rather tired,' Alison acknowledged, feeling as if she'd just run a marathon. 'But, I was wondering . . . how long will I have to stay in the hospital?'

'I think a couple of days would be in order,' Nick answered. 'There are some tests I'd like to run.'

'Tests? What kind of tests?' Alison asked, feeling her anxiety return.

'If you'll excuse me, I'll leave Nick to explain,' Dr. Jacobson cut in. 'I'll pop in and see you tomorrow, Alison, if I may?' He glanced at her.

'Yes, please do,' she responded, managing a smile, deciding that she liked Dr. Jacobson, his warm manner and his smile.

But when the door closed behind him, the realization that she was alone with her husband sent a shiver of apprehension chasing along her spine.

'Don't look so worried, Alison. I'm not going to eat you,' Nick said, and at his comment her glance flew to meet his in time to glimpse a spark of anger in the depths of his eyes.

'It's all so strange,' she said, almost to herself. 'I mean, I don't remember being married.' She drew a steadying breath. 'Are you really my husband?' she asked, unable to hold back the question.

Nick's eyes flashed to hers and Alison felt her whole body tense in fearful anticipation.

She scanned his features. Searching . . . for what? She wasn't quite sure. But all she could think about was the fact that when he'd entered her room earlier he hadn't greeted her as a man would greet the woman he loved. He hadn't rushed to her side, kissed her or hugged her, or in any way exhibited that he was glad to see her or relieved that she was all right.

His manner had been strictly professional, with no indication that there was a relationship of any kind between them.

'Yes. I'm your husband. We are legally married,' Nick told her in a decisive tone, leaving her in no doubt that he was speaking the truth. But his attitude left her wondering if perhaps all was not well between them.

Again she found herself struggling with conflicting emotions as a multitude of questions sprang to life within her. How had they met? Where had they met? How long had they been married? *Did* they have any children? Was their marriage in trouble? Surely they must have been in love . . .

She looked down at her hands twisting at the bedcovers. 'I wish I could remember — ' She broke off, her throat clogging with emotion.

Suddenly Nick's hand came up to cup her chin. His touch sent her pulse into a frenzy and it was all she could do to meet his eyes. The look of tenderness she could see in their depths left her feeling weak and more than a little breathless.

'I know this is difficult for you, Alison.' His voice was cool and oddly comforting. 'But it's not exactly easy for me, either.'

She felt like a doe trapped in the headlights of a car as his gaze held her captive. For the life of her she couldn't move, and as the seconds ticked by, an earthy masculine scent began to slowly wrap itself around her and an unfamiliar heat began to spread through her.

She had the strongest urge to reach out and touch Nick's cheek, to feel the texture of his skin, then run her fingers through his thick black hair. If she gave in to the need coursing through her, would the barriers surrounding her mind melt away? The question danced into her head, enticing her to close the gap between them.

The air seemed to quiver with anticipation and excitement and Alison found herself inching closer, as though she was under a hypnotic spell.

The knock on the hospital room door shattered the silence, startling them both. Alison drew back as though she'd been stung, and Nick's hand fell to his side.

'Excuse me, Dr. Montgomery.' The voice belonged to Nurse Lucas. 'Miss Jennings is here to see you. She's waiting in your office,' the woman explained.

Several seconds passed before Nick answered. 'Thank you. Tell her I'll be right there.'

The nurse nodded and withdrew.

'Alison, I have to go.' Nick was already backing away.

'Of course . . . I understand,' Alison replied, keeping her gaze averted.

'I'll be back as soon as I can.' He came to a halt at the door. 'In the meantime, try to get some rest. And don't worry about those tests, they're strictly routine,' he assured her.

'Thanks,' she replied, throwing him a grateful glance.

'I know everything must be confusing for you,' Nick said evenly. 'And I know you have a lot of questions you want to ask. But remember, Rome wasn't built in a day.' His mouth curled in a smile that tugged at her heartstrings.

She could only nod in response.

'I'll be back,' he said, and with that he was gone.

Closing her eyes, Alison let the silence settle over her like a comforting blanket. Tears stung the back of her eyes and she was sorely tempted to give in to the urge to cry. Several solitary tears slid through her lashes and she quickly wiped them away.

What would have happened if the nurse hadn't interrupted? she wondered. Would Nick have kissed her? The question brought a warmth to her cheeks as well as feelings of both restlessness and regret.

If they were husband and wife — Her

thoughts came to a halt. There was no if. Nicholas Montgomery *was* her husband. Why would he lie? And besides, the awareness that fizzled between them, and her body's response to his nearness, were strong indications that they'd already shared more than a kiss.

At this thought a shiver chased down her spine and a tingling heat spread through her. Well, at least she hadn't forgotten what it was like to be a woman: her feminine instincts, responses and reactions were all working normally.

The swish of the door opening broke into her thoughts and she glanced up to see Nurse Lucas enter, carrying towels and a basin.

'I thought you might want to freshen up a little,' she said with a smile.

'That would be nice, thank you,' Alison replied.

'Are you hungry?' Nurse Lucas asked as she placed the basin on the table in front of Alison.

'Thirsty, actually,' Alison said, realizing that her throat was very dry.

'How does a glass of ice-cold apple juice sound?'

'Terrific.' Alison smiled.

'First things first. My instructions are to remove your intravenous,' the nurse said as she reached for Alison's right hand. 'There! That should be more comfortable for you.' She gathered up the tube and lifted the bag with the clear liquid from the stand next to the bed.

'Thanks,' Alison said as she picked up the facecloth provided and dipped it into the basin of warm water.

Nurse Lucas paused when she reached the door. 'If you lift up the center piece of your table you'll find a mirror.'

Alison froze momentarily at the nurse's words, then with great deliberation she squeezed the water out of the cloth. With gentle strokes she skimmed the surface of her face, but her glance kept returning to the table and the hidden mirror.

Taking a deep breath, Alison set the

cloth aside and lifted the center section of the table. The person staring back at her had skin as pale as chalk and a look of childlike fragility.

Chocolate brown, shoulder-length hair, with bangs falling across her forehead, framed a face that was oval in shape. Alison guessed the age of the woman staring back at her to be somewhere in her early twenties.

Pretty but not beautiful, she thought as she studied her features one by one. Dark brown eyebrows curved above brown eyes that held a mixture of curiosity and longing. The high cheekbones could be considered attractive, but her nose was too short and her mouth too big, she decided critically.

She watched in fascination as the lower lip in the mirror began to tremble, then the mouth opened to reveal even white teeth.

As she continued to gaze at her reflection, she noted that the anxious expression in the brown eyes perfectly matched the emotions churning inside her.

The slow inspection had garnered no response from within, no leap of her pulse, no flash of recognition, no recollection from her past, and the hope she'd harbored that seeing herself might jolt her memory, faded and died.

As feelings of despair washed over her, the image of the stranger in the mirror began to blur. Anger and frustration had her blinking away the tears, and none too gently she dropped the mirror back into its hiding place.

She would not cry. She would not cry! She repeated the litany over and over inside her head. Besides, tears weren't the answer. Sometime in the next hour or day, or week, her memory would return. It was all she could hope for. She had to believe it!

Nurse Lucas returned, bringing a glass of apple juice, and Alison managed a smile of welcome. With firm determination she set aside her fears and anxieties.

'How long have I been in the hospital?' she asked.

'Ah . . . you were brought in late Saturday afternoon,' the nurse told her.

'What day is it today?' Alison asked.

'Monday.' Nurse Lucas eyed her curiously. 'So it is true. You really don't remember anything?'

'Nothing,' Alison replied.

'How awful!'

'It does make life a little difficult,' Alison agreed, a hint of humor in her tone.

'Oh boy . . . I forgot!' Nurse Lucas exclaimed. 'Dr. Jacobson told us not to answer any questions.'

'I doubt that telling me what day it is will have any adverse effect on my recovery,' Alison said lightly. 'Would you mind opening the blinds?' she went on, suddenly curious to know what the weather was like, and whether it was spring, summer, fall or winter — things generally taken for granted.

'Be happy to. Just let me take the basin out of your way.' The nurse lifted the basin onto the table before pushing it to the foot of the bed. Crossing to the window, she opened the blinds.

Outside the sky was just beginning to grow dark as evening slowly descended. The hospital parking lot, half filled with cars, stretched out below, and the tall lamp standards spaced at intervals throughout the lot were on, illuminating the area and giving it a reddish glow.

'Bayview.' Alison spoke the name aloud. 'Is that the name of the town as well as the hospital?' she asked, recalling the answer the nurse had given her earlier.

'Yes,' Nurse Lucas replied.

'Where exactly is Bayview?' Alison asked.

'Ah . . . maybe I'd better get your husband . . . I mean, Dr. Montgomery.' The woman was obviously unwilling to answer too many questions.

'Bayview is on the Washington coast, north of Seattle.'

Alison instantly recognized the deep,

rich tones and her glance flew across the room. Her stomach tightened at the sight of her husband standing in the doorway. She swallowed convulsively and fought to steady her erratic pulse.

He truly was the most incredibly handsome man she'd ever seen, but she noticed this time that there were lines of strain around his eyes and mouth. Fleetingly she remembered the nurse saying he'd spent the past two nights in the chair by her bed.

'If you'll excuse me.' Nurse Lucas crossed to the bed to retrieve the basin and towels from the table.

'Does Seattle ring any bells?' Nick asked once the nurse had departed.

Alison dropped her gaze and tried to concentrate. After a lengthy pause, she spoke. 'Seattle is a city in the state of Washington in the northwest corner of the United States.' Her voice rose excitedly. 'To the east is Idaho, to the south, Oregon, and to the north, Canada. In 1962, the World's Fair was held in Seattle and the Space Needle was one of the main attractions,' she concluded, thrilled to discover that she knew Seattle and, more important, that she remembered something.

'Well done!' Nick crossed to stand by the bed. 'You've just taken the first step toward a full recovery.' He followed his words with a smile.

The smile sent her senses reeling and her head spinning, making her aware once more of the reaction she had to this man.

'What about Bayview? Do you remember that, too?' he asked, breaking into her thoughts. Alison closed her eyes and channeled all her energy on the name Bayview. She was sure that an image like the one that had flashed before her when she thought of Seattle would materialize in her mind.

She was met with nothing. Nothing but blackness. The elation she'd felt only a moment ago burst like a soap bubble and the headache that had diminished considerably with the aid of the medication, throbbed insistently to life once more.

Her hand moved to massage the bridge of her nose and across her forehead, and suddenly Nick touched her shoulder.

'Don't try to force it,' he said, his words drifting through the pain, and there was no mistaking the concern in his voice. But strangely Alison was actually thinking about Nick, about the way he greeted her each time he appeared. There was concern, yes, but beneath the concern was a definite caution, and Alison was at a loss to understand it. He treated her as a doctor would an ordinary patient, not the way a husband would treat a wife.

Something was wrong. Instinctively Alison sensed that their relationship was not idyllic. Were they separated? Or perhaps in the throes of a divorce?

'Ours isn't a happy marriage, is it?' She blurted out the question and felt Nick's hand tighten at her shoulder for a moment before he removed it.

Fighting down the feeling of helplessness, she lifted her eyes to meet his, but his expression was carefully masked, his dark eyes giving nothing away. If only she could remember! Frustration had her gritting her teeth.

'Why don't you answer my question?' she asked, relieved that her voice remained steady.

'Alison . . . ' Nick cautioned, and she could hear the strain in his voice. 'Dr. Jacobson advised that it would be better if you were allowed to remember things in your own time. I have to abide by his recommendation.'

I must be right, Alison thought despairingly. She dropped her gaze to the bedcovers and began to trace a pattern with her fingers, all the while wishing she hadn't pushed for his reply.

'Tonight, I suggest you rest and try not to worry.' Nick's tone was very brusque and businesslike, that of a doctor talking to his patient. 'You suffered rather a nasty blow to your head, but apart from that there are only a few bruises. Tomorrow I'll run some routine tests and who knows, maybe by then you'll remember everything,' he concluded brightly.

'I hope so.' Alison's voice was little more than a whisper.

His hand covered hers and at the contact a jolt of electricity ricocheted along her arm, as if she'd touched a live wire.

Startled, she jerked free, glancing up in time to see a look of annoyance flash in Nick's eyes before he turned away. Confusion and sympathy had her reaching out to him but he'd already moved away and Alison's hand merely floated briefly in midair, before coming to rest on the bedcovers.

'I think it's best if I leave now.' He came to a halt at the door. 'Is there anything I can get for you before I go?' he asked, turning to face her.

'No, I'm fine, thank you,' she said, noticing the weariness in his stance.

'Good night, Alison.' He spoke softly, the low timbre of his voice strangely soothing. 'See you in the morning,' he added, and with that he was gone.

Alison sat staring at the door for several long moments. Again she found herself thinking that Nick's behavior was a far cry from that of a man who said he was her husband, a man supposedly in love with his wife.

A good-night kiss would have been in order, ordinarily. But there was nothing ordinary about this situation or, for that matter, about Nicholas Montgomery.

He hadn't answered her question. He'd made a point of avoiding it and she felt reasonably safe in assuming that his reluctance stemmed from the fact that she'd hit a nerve, that what she'd said about their marriage was true.

What other explanation could there be? she asked herself. And it seemed logical that he wouldn't want to tell her she was right. As a doctor his first obligation was to ensure that the patients' welfare wasn't jeopardized in any way.

She glanced down at the plain gold band on her finger and began to twist it. She wore no engagement ring. Did that mean the nursing staff had removed it, or that she'd never been given one?

Not every woman wore an engagement ring, she rationalized. Some simply chose a wide wedding band and often had an inscription engraved on the inside. At this thought Alison tried to slide the band off her finger, but when it reached her knuckle, the ring refused to budge.

With a weary sigh, she closed her eyes.

How long would it be before her memory returned? she wondered. Only then would she learn the truth about her relationship with Nick. Was their marriage in trouble? *Had* they drifted apart? Suddenly, for the first time since she'd awakened, Alison wasn't altogether sure she wanted to know the answers.

3

She was running down a dark, narrow hallway. She couldn't tell if she was in a house, a hotel or an apartment. The floor was carpeted and felt springy beneath her feet. Ahead of her was a door, partially opened, and she could hear the sound of muffled voices coming from within.

She slowed to a halt, puzzled by the fact that though she'd been running for several minutes, she seemed no nearer to the door than when she'd started. She continued to make her way down the hallway driven by curiosity and a growing need to know who was talking.

The voices grew louder, more insistent. One was a man's and the other a woman's, but she couldn't make out what they were saying.

Suddenly the sound of someone sobbing rent the air, but though she renewed her efforts to reach the door, she couldn't get any closer. The more she tried, the farther away the door appeared to be.

Heart pounding, she slowed to a halt and a gray fog began to swirl around her, making it difficult to see. She closed her eyes for a moment and when she opened them again she was startled to discover that she was now standing directly in front of the door.

The crying had ceased, replaced by the sound of a man's voice, deep and low and vaguely familiar. But his words were drawn out and indistinguishable, like a record on an old gramophone that hadn't been wound up properly.

She lifted her hand to push open the door, but before she could touch it, she felt someone tug at her skirt. Glancing down, she saw a small child with bright blue eyes and long blond hair smiling up at her.

'Sara!' The name erupted from Alison's lips and she awoke with a start, sitting bolt upright in bed. Her heart was pounding against her breast and she was gasping for breath, as though she'd just run a mile. Her body was wet with perspiration and she glanced around the dimly lit room in total confusion.

Several minutes ticked by before her breathing returned to normal, but with it came the memory of waking up the previous evening and all that had ensued since then.

With a moan of frustration, Alison lay back against the pillows. She was still a woman without a past. Though she'd spent a peaceful night, at least most of it, Dr. Jacobson's inference that she might wake up remembering everything hadn't come to pass.

But she *had* remembered something — no, Alison corrected herself, she'd remembered some*one* — and as this realization registered, her spirits lifted.

Sara! She was sure Sara was the name of the child in her dream, the child who'd tugged at her skirt. Perhaps she could conjure up the young girl's image again.

Alison closed her eyes and tried to relax. If she could only drift back to sleep, back to the dream, to that level of consciousness just below wakefulness.

Squeezing her eyes tightly now, Alison tried to replay those moments prior to waking, but after repeated attempts she was forced to acknowledge that the door through which the memory had escaped had closed again.

But who was Sara? A sister? A niece? Or, she drew a steadying breath, a daughter! Alison felt her stomach muscles clench at the thought that the child might well be her own flesh and blood. But surely she would recognize her own daughter? How could a woman forget giving birth?

Feelings of guilt washed over Alison and a pain stabbed at her heart. Fighting back tears, she threw the bedcovers aside and stood up.

She wasn't an invalid. Apart from the bump on her head she had no broken bones or any life-threatening injuries.

She couldn't stay here. She had to get out. She had to do something! But first she needed to find her clothes. She must have been wearing clothes when she was brought in.

After she got dressed she would take a walk outside, and perhaps see someone or something that would trigger her memory. It was worth a try.

Glancing around, she spotted a locker on the opposite side of the room. Her legs felt like two pieces of straw and she had to stand next to the bed for several minutes, gathering energy, annoyed and frustrated that she should feel so weak.

Squaring her shoulders, she focused her attention on the locker. Her clothes had to be in there, she thought as she took first one step, and then another.

She'd managed two more steps before the door to her room opened.

'Alison! Good heavens, woman. Are you crazy?' Nick's voice shattered the silence, sending shock waves ricocheting through her. His sudden appearance robbed her of what little strength she had and she began to crumple like a rag doll.

Strong arms caught her almost before she knew she was falling and she found herself being lifted into Nick's arms and held tightly against his muscular chest.

Her arms instinctively went around his neck and as she breathed in his evocative, male scent she felt something stir to life deep inside her, like a butterfly's first movement as it awakens and begins to emerge from its cocoon.

Her head nestled comfortably against the curve of his throat, and she could see a sprinkling of dark hairs at the vee of his open-necked shirt.

Through the thin covering of the hospital gown she wore she could feel his hands where he held her; at her thigh, just above her knees, and under her arm.

At each point of contact she was

aware of a heat radiating inward and with it a strange longing.

With a sigh, Alison closed her eyes and gave herself up to the unmistakable feeling that this was where she belonged.

Had he held her this way before? she wondered as he carried her toward the bed. What other explanation could there be for the fact that she felt so utterly safe in his arms? And surely if they were man and wife it wasn't unreasonable to assume that he had carried her to bed before.

At this thought Alison felt her face grow hot and her pulse gathered momentum as a tingling sensation danced across her nerve endings.

'Just where were you planning to go?' Nick asked as he lowered her gently onto the bed.

Alison reluctantly released her hold on him and waited for her pulse to return to normal. Through lowered lashes, she watched as Nick reached into the pocket of his white coat and extracted a small penlight.

Leaning over her, he proceeded to shine the light into her eyes. After several seconds he drew away.

'You didn't answer my question,' he said, a coaxing note in his voice.

She hesitated for a moment. 'I . . . just wanted to get out of here,' she responded.

'Something wrong with the service?' he asked jokingly, his mouth curling into a smile.

Alison didn't respond and as the silence lengthened she felt a tension simmering in the air. 'Who's Sara?' Her question broke the silence and at her words Nick's smile vanished and an emotion she couldn't decipher flashed in the depths of his dark eyes.

'Has your memory come back?' His tone was urgent, and Alison noticed the pulse throbbing at his jaw.

She shook her head. 'No . . . I had a dream . . . and there was a small child . . . I think her name is Sara,' she explained.

'Tell me about the dream,' Nick said evenly, though the tension was still evident in his stance.

'There isn't much to tell,' she said.

'Humor me,' he replied, but there was an edge to his voice Alison found disconcerting.

She swallowed and to give herself some breathing space, she squirmed beneath the bedcovers, clutching the blankets in both hands and pulling them up to her chin.

Nick stood over her, silently waiting for her to speak. From outside in the corridor came a variety of sounds; the clatter of dishes, the squeak of a trolley. Suddenly the aroma of brewed coffee wafted into the room and her stomach churned noisily as she felt the first pangs of hunger.

She glanced up at Nick in the hope that he'd offer to get her a cup of coffee, but as she met his gaze his eyes seemed to bore into hers, almost as if he was trying to see inside her head.

Taking a deep breath, she began. 'I

dreamt I was walking along a hallway . . . a carpeted hallway,' she amended. 'I don't know where, a house, I think.'

'And . . . ' Nick prompted.

Alison closed her eyes, trying to replay the scene that had floated into her mind earlier. 'I could hear voices, a man's and a woman's. They were coming from behind a door. But I couldn't hear what they were saying. I finally reached the door and was just about to push it open when someone tugged at my skirt. I looked down and saw this child . . . ' The child's angelic features flashed before her once more. 'The name Sara just popped into my head,' she concluded, opening her eyes.

'And that's all?' Nick asked.

'Yes,' Alison replied. 'Is Sara our daughter?' she asked, but Nick didn't appear to have heard the question, his thoughts obviously elsewhere.

Suddenly another thought struck Alison, sending an icy fear chasing down her spine. 'Was she with me . . . I mean, was the child with me when I was hurt?' Concern had her reaching out to grasp Nick's arm. 'Was she hurt? Tell me. I have to know.' Her voice wavered with emotion.

'Sara's fine, believe me. She's just fine,' Nick assured her, taking her hand in his.

Relief washed over Alison like a summer shower, dispelling the fear instantly. 'Please tell me about her. Who is she?'

'Sara's my niece,' Nick told her, but before he could say more the door opened and a hospital orderly holding a breakfast tray appeared in the doorway.

'Oh . . . excuse me. I didn't know you were here, Doctor.' The orderly came to a halt. 'I'll just leave the tray,' she added, setting it on the table at the foot of the bed.

'Thank you,' Alison said, trying not to feel annoyed by the untimely interruption.

'Breakfast smells good.' Nick reached for the table and pulled it toward Alison. Lifting the cover from the tray, he revealed a plate of scrambled eggs and two slices of brown toast. A glass of orange juice and another of milk, together with a bowl of cereal, took up the remaining space.

As the aroma from the food assailed her senses, Alison's stomach rumbled in a sharp reminder that she was hungry.

The door swung open once more, and Alison glanced up to see a nurse this time. 'Dr. Montgomery, I'm sorry to disturb you, but the orderly told me you were in here.'

'What is it, Nurse Cramer?' Nick asked.

'Miss Jennings is here. She's rather upset . . . ' The nurse hesitated, throwing a fleeting glance at Alison. 'Ah . . . she insisted that I track you down, sir.'

'Tell her I'll be right there,' Nick said, and waited for the nurse to leave before turning to Alison. 'I'm sorry, but duty calls. Occupational hazard, I'm afraid,' he added. 'We'll talk later.' He strode toward the door. 'By the way,' he said, his hand on the doorknob. 'I've made arrangements for you to have those routine tests this morning.'

'Will I be able to leave the hospital today?' Alison asked.

'We'll see,' he replied. 'If you pass the tests with flying colors, and I'm sure you will, there's really no reason to keep you here,' he told her. 'But I'd like to check with Dr. Jacobson on that. Unfortunately I'll be in surgery for most of the morning. I'll drop by as soon as I can. Enjoy your breakfast,' he added, and with that he was gone.

Alison fought down the feelings of frustration that surfaced. Reaching for the toast on the plate, she bit into the bread and began, thoughtfully, to chew.

It seemed that every time Nick was about to divulge something interesting, something that might trigger her memory, he was distracted.

She frowned and picked up the fork from the tray. He'd told her Sara was his niece, but while that knowledge brought Alison a sense of relief, she still wanted to know more about the child. The fact that she'd remembered Sara might be significant.

During those moments in her dream when she'd seen the young girl's face, Alison had sensed that there was a strong bond between them.

Was it true? If so, how had the bond been established? Had Sara been staying with them before the accident?

There were so many questions still unanswered. Alison sighed and, unable to ignore her body's hunger pangs any longer, returned her attention to the food on the tray.

For the next few minutes she concentrated on appeasing that hunger, and when the nurse returned to collect the breakfast tray, there were only a few crumbs left on the plate.

'Would you like to freshen up?' the woman asked her. 'I could bring you a basin with water, or maybe you might feel up to taking a bath this morning?'

'A bath would be heavenly,' Alison said with heartfelt enthusiasm. 'But will

I be able to wash my hair?' Lifting her hand, she ran her fingers through her hair, gently probing the injured area, relieved to discover that the swelling had gone down markedly.

'I don't think that's a good idea,' the nurse advised. 'Sorry. Perhaps tomorrow,' she suggested.

'Fine,' Alison replied, already longing to step into a tub of hot water. 'What about the tests Dr. Montgomery mentioned?'

'The orderly who will escort you won't be down for another hour,' the nurse said. 'I'll run you a bath right now.'

Five minutes later Alison slowly lowered herself into the steaming tub of water and breathed a sigh of contentment. She'd twisted her hair into a knot on the side of her head and secured it with a clip in an effort to keep it dry. She was tempted for a moment to disobey the nurse and shampoo her hair, but the hot water quickly sapped her energy, even as it soothed.

Apart from the bump on her head and a general feeling of weakness, she felt fine physically. But when she'd asked Nick about being released, she hadn't thought the situation through. She'd forgotten one important consideration. Getting out of the hospital meant going home . . . with her husband.

Alison quickly diverted her thoughts away from Nick and turned her attention to trying to remember something . . . anything.

Bayview. Was it a small town or a large city? Judging by the brief glimpse she'd had from the window of her hospital room, she guessed the community was relatively small.

She lived in Bayview with her husband — Alison muttered under her breath, annoyed that her thoughts had once again returned to Nick.

But Nick Montgomery was much too distracting, she decided, recalling those moments when he'd scooped her into his arms and carried her back to the bed.

And he was her husband! A sweet rush of excitement swept over her, leaving a tingling heat in its wake. How on earth had she come to be married to a man as handsome and exciting as Nicholas Montgomery?

Irritated with her reaction, she reached for the soap and quickly worked up a lather, focusing on the task at hand, determined not to think of Nick.

A few minutes later Alison slowly sank into the water to rinse off, her mind dutifully turned to the problem of her forgotten past.

Had she been born in Bayview? Grown up in the area? Attended school here? No. She shook her head in firm denial. Just as her inner instinct had told her earlier that she had no family, now it was telling her that Bayview wasn't her hometown.

Then it must be Nick's, she reasoned. Had he brought her here as a bride? How had they met? Nick was a doctor. It was logical that she'd met him in a working situation. Was she a

58

doctor or a nurse?

Alison held her breath for a moment. She was beginning to have faith in her own gut instincts, but this time there was no overwhelming feeling that she was on the right track.

How *had* they met? The fact that she couldn't remember bothered her a great deal. The man was unforgettable. Each time he was near, each time she thought of him, she was made aware of her reaction to him, a reaction that certainly seemed to indicate there was something between them . . . and yet . . .

Closing her eyes, she had no difficulty whatsoever conjuring up Nick's strong, dynamic features. She guessed his age to be about forty, but there was no hint of gray in the hair that was as black as coal. His face seemed almost chiseled out of granite, but there was compassion and kindness in the depth of his eyes.

Alison sighed as she drifted off into a dreamlike state.

Suddenly a picture flashed into her

mind. An image of a man and a woman wrapped in each other's arms.

The man was Nick. There was no mistaking those handsome features, the taut jawline, the aristocratic nose, those incredible eyes.

And the woman? Coppery red, stylishly cut hair framed a face that was classic in its beauty.

For a brief moment a memory danced on the edges of Alison's mind, tantalizingly close, but like a star falling from the sky it vanished before she could grasp it.

Pain began to throb at her temples and, shivering now, she opened her eyes and climbed out onto the cold tile floor. Reaching for the towel hanging on the rail, she wrapped it around herself in an attempt to restore some warmth to her chilled body.

Who was the beautiful woman in Nick's arms? A friend . . . or a lover?

4

Friend or *lover*. The words echoed through Alison's head but no answer came. Nick was her husband, and yet some inner instinct told her all was not well between them. Could the reason have something to do with the red-haired woman?

Suddenly a knock on the bathroom door brought Alison out of her dazed state.

'Mrs. Montgomery? Are you all right?'

Alison blinked and a shudder danced through her body as she hugged the towel tightly around her.

'Yes, I'm fine.' Deliberately she put her troubled thoughts on hold. With trembling hands she slowly tried to rub some warmth back into her frozen limbs.

'The orderly will be here in a few minutes to take you down for those tests,' the nurse informed her.

'Thank you. I'll be right out,' Alison replied, wishing she could lock the door and shut out the world, at least until her memory returned.

With a sigh she let the towel fall and retrieved the clean hospital gown from the chair nearby. As she slid her arms into the gown she caught a glimpse of her reflection in the mirror above the sink.

The face of the woman looking back at her was pale and drawn and etched with strain. Staring at the features, Alison held her breath for a moment, hoping once more for a flash of recognition, anything that would take away the expression of pain and despair she could see in the depths of her brown eyes.

Nothing. Lifting a hand to her hair, Alison removed the clip that held it in place and let the heavy swath tumble to her shoulders.

She ran her fingers through the thick mass, trying to comb it into some semblance of order, careful to avoid the swelling at the back of her head.

Surely the brief flashes of memory she'd been experiencing were an indication that in time her memory would indeed return!

Hope flickered briefly in her eyes. She would just have to take it slow — hour by hour, day by day. Alison drew a steadying breath and, turning from the mirror, made her way out of the bathroom.

'There you are.' The nurse had just finished tucking in the covers on the bed. 'Feel better?' she asked with a friendly smile.

Alison managed to nod and smile, warmed by the genuine concern she could hear in the nurse's voice.

'I'm sure Dr. Montgomery brought in a housecoat for you.' The nurse crossed to the locker. 'Here it is,' she went on, turning to show her a beautiful royal blue velour robe.

As Alison slid her arms into the robe and tightened the sash a feeling of comfort and warmth stole over her, effectively dispelling the chill. She knew instinctively the robe was hers, and as her fingers stroked the smooth material she felt strangely at peace.

A knock sounded and the door swung open to reveal a man in his mid-thirties, with light brown hair and blue eyes, dressed in white pants and jacket.

He pushed an empty wheelchair into the room and came to a halt just inside the door. He flashed a smile at the nurse, then turned to Alison. 'Mrs. Montgomery?'

'Yes,' she acknowledged, thinking fleetingly that her response to the name was already becoming automatic.

'Your chariot awaits, madam.' The orderly made a sweeping motion with his hand toward the wheelchair.

Alison smiled. 'Thank you,' she said, moving to occupy the chair, finding herself suddenly eager to leave the confines of her room, eager to explore the hospital. Perhaps the outing would even jog her memory.

'We're off.' The man deftly opened the door with one hand and maneuvered her out into the corridor.

Less than an hour later, after paying a visit to the X-ray department and the lab where a technician expertly and painlessly extracted a vial of blood for testing, Alison was once more back in her hospital room.

Instead of lifting her spirits, however, the tour had left her feeling discouraged. She'd received friendly greetings from almost everyone they'd encountered as the orderly accompanied her from one floor to the next, but nothing and no one had seemed familiar and the only conclusion Alison reached as she was wheeled back into her room was that she wasn't overly fond of hospitals.

A lunch tray with vegetable soup and a tuna sandwich had been left for her, but she was too restless and impatient to eat, her mind preoccupied with finding the answers to the growing list of questions circling inside her head.

But while she was anxious to fill in the missing pieces of her life, she also acknowledged that there was a part of her that shied away from uncovering the past.

Crossing to the window, she stood gazing out at the people and cars coming and going below. The sound of an ambulance siren, at first faint then growing ever louder, could be heard as it approached the hospital.

Alison quickly located the vehicle with its lights flashing and watched its progress until it turned into the hospital driveway. Tires squealed loudly in protest as it sped around the corner before coming to a halt in front of the emergency entrance.

The screech of tires sent a shiver chasing down her spine and with it an eerie sense of déjà vu. Had she been brought to the hospital by ambulance?

Alison closed her eyes and immediately a blurry image danced at the outer edges of her consciousness. Heart pounding, she tried to concentrate on bringing the image into focus, but the harder she tried, the blurrier the picture became.

With a moan of despair she leaned her forehead against the window, finding the touch of the cold glass on her brow oddly soothing.

Suddenly the memory that had been so evasive only moments before flashed with vivid clarity into her mind. She was hurrying down a paved driveway, heading toward a set of wrought-iron gates. The gates stood open, and without bothering to slow down, she ran out into the street. Instantly the squeal of tires shattered the silence and a quick glance to the left revealed a car skidding toward her.

'Alison?'

At the sound of her name, Alison let out a yelp of surprise and jumped back, an action that caused her to collide with Nick, whose entry and approach she hadn't heard.

'Hey! Take it easy.' Nick grabbed her shoulders in an attempt to steady her.

Glancing up at him, Alison met his gaze, and seeing the genuine look of concern in the depth of those fathomless dark eyes, she felt her breath catch in her throat and a shiver of awareness chase across her nerve endings.

'I'm sorry,' she said a little breathlessly, unsure for a moment whether Nick himself, or the fright she'd received as a result of his unexpected appearance, was the reason for her agitation.

He wore a pale green tunic and matching pants, an outfit she'd seen a number of times during her earlier tour. But somehow the rather drab attire only served to accentuate the width of his shoulders and breadth of his chest.

'I'm the one who should be apologizing,' he said evenly. 'I didn't mean to startle you.' His gaze skimmed over her face. 'What is it?' he hurried on. 'You look like you've seen a ghost.'

'I — I think I remembered something,' she said, and at her words an expression she couldn't quite decipher came and went in his eyes.

'Tell me,' he urged gently, his breath fanning her face in a light caress.

'It isn't much.' She swallowed and took a step back, finding his nearness more than a little distracting.

'I'd still like to know,' he countered, and Alison heard the hint of frustration in his voice.

She took another step back, noting as she did, the frown that darkened Nick's features.

Dropping her gaze, she tugged on the sash of her robe and drew a steadying breath before continuing. 'I was running down a driveway, heading toward some wrought-iron gates,' she told him, thinking as she spoke that perhaps in recounting the tale she might jar free another forgotten piece of her life. 'I ran past the gates and out onto the road and suddenly I heard the screech of brakes — ' She broke off and glanced once more at Nick, in time to see a look of horror flash briefly in his eyes.

'That's it? That's all you remember?'

He met her gaze now with an intensity that sent a ripple of excitement coursing through her.

'Yes, that's all I remember,' she confirmed, trying with difficulty to ignore the erratic beat of her pulse. 'Did the car hit me? Is that what happened? Was that the reason I was brought here?' she quickly asked.

Nick remained silent and she could almost see the internal struggle going on in the depths of his eyes.

'Why was I running? Where was I going? What was I running from?' Alison fired the questions at him in rapid succession, hoping to badger him into giving her a truthful response.

He held her gaze for several long seconds before he spoke. 'I've been asking myself those same questions.' There was no mistaking the underlying anger and frustration in his voice.

'What do you mean?' Alison asked, surprised by his reply.

Nick dropped his gaze and turned away, tension in every line of his body.

Raking a hand through his hair, he sighed, then swung around to face her once more. 'I have no idea why you ran out of the house and into the street,' he told her in a tightly controlled voice. 'That the car didn't hit you is a miracle in itself. But somehow the driver managed to stop in time.' He inhaled deeply before continuing. 'He told me you simply collapsed under his wheels, hitting your head on the edge of the sidewalk as you fell.'

'He told you? You mean you were there?' Alison quickly focused on his words.

'Yes, I was there.' Nick's hand came up to rub the back of his neck. He closed his eyes for a moment and Alison held her breath, silently urging him to tell her more.

'The driveway you were running down . . . ' He opened his eyes and a look of indecision flitted across his face.

'Leads to your house,' Alison supplied.

His eyes flashed to hers. 'You remember?'

She shook her head in denial. 'Just a

guess.' At her words a look of relief danced briefly in his eyes, but before she could pursue the subject, there was a knock on the door and it opened to reveal Dr. Jacobson.

'Hello, Alison,' Dr. Jacobson greeted her. 'Why, Nick! I didn't expect to find you here. I thought you were assisting Dr. Conroy.'

'I did,' Nick said. 'But Dennis had to reschedule Mrs. Kawalski. She came down with an infection,' he explained.

'That's too bad,' Dr. Jacobson responded. 'But now it leaves you free to take your wife home.'

'I'm being released?' Alison couldn't hide her surprise.

'Indeed you are,' Dr. Jacobson replied. 'Your X rays were all clear and the lab results on those blood tests came up normal. Everything checks out just fine.'

'Oh . . . I see . . . ' Alison stopped, feeling her face grow warm. 'I mean . . . that's great,' she hurried on, aware of Nick's eyes on her.

'There's every reason to believe that

once you're home amid surroundings that were once familiar to you, the chances of a complete recovery are high,' Dr. Jacobson explained. 'But, please, don't expect miracles, and don't be discouraged if it should take days or even weeks,' he cautioned.

Alison nodded, wishing she felt as confident as Dr. Jacobson. 'Thank you,' she added politely.

'Just try not to force things,' the older doctor advised. 'And I'd like to see you in about a week. But in the meantime, please feel free to call me, or come in and see me anytime.'

'I will.' Alison managed a smile.

'Try not to worry,' Dr. Jacobson continued. 'Things will sort themselves out. I know Nick is anxious to have you home, and believe me you couldn't be in better hands.'

'You've been very kind.' Alison kept her attention focused on the older man, careful to avoid making eye contact with Nick.

For a moment she was tempted to

tell Dr. Jacobson about the brief flashes of memory she'd been experiencing, but while she'd told Nick about two of those flashes, she hadn't mentioned the third — the one where she'd seen him in the arms of another woman.

'Take care.' Dr. Jacobson's voice effectively cut through her wayward thoughts. 'I've signed the necessary paperwork so you can leave whenever you're ready,' he added, and with a smile and a wave he was gone.

The door closed behind Dr. Jacobson, leaving Alison once again alone with the man who was her husband. Under normal circumstances, being given a clean bill of health and told she could go home would have been cause for celebration. Instead Alison was aware of a tension within her that was becoming increasingly difficult to ignore.

'Your clothes are in the locker,' Nick said, breaking the silence. 'I'll leave you to get dressed. I'll be back in twenty minutes. I want to stop by my office and make a couple of phone calls.'

'Fine,' Alison said evenly, determined not to let him see that she wasn't exactly looking forward to the prospect of going home with him.

Suddenly Nick moved to stand in front of her. 'Look, I know this must be difficult for you, and correct me if I'm wrong, but I get the impression you'd really rather stay here at the hospital a little longer.' He paused for a moment. 'If you want to stay, believe me, I'll understand,' he told her softly.

Alison felt a lump form in her throat at the tenderness and understanding she could hear in his voice. She swallowed. 'I do feel a bit over-whelmed,' she said, still unsure about what she should do.

'I told Sara this morning that you probably wouldn't be coming home for another day or two,' Nick continued.

Alison felt the blood rush to her face as a wave of guilt washed over her at the mention of the child. How could she have forgotten about Sara? 'How is Sara?' she asked quickly. 'Does she

know? I mean . . . Did you explain — '
Alison broke off.

'That you've lost your memory?' Nick
quickly filled in the remainder of her
question. 'Yes, I told her,' he said. 'But
she's only five. I'm not sure she under-
stands what 'losing your memory' means.'

'Where is she now? At home?' Alison
asked, her curiosity about the child
steadily growing.

'No,' Nick replied with a shake of his
dark head. 'She's staying with her
friend, Katie. I thought I'd call her and
tell her you were coming home. She
misses you,' he went on. 'I've tried to
reassure her, but I think she's anxious
to see for herself that you're all right.'

Alison heard the hint of weariness in
Nick's voice and for the first time she
found herself thinking of the toll
her accident and subsequent loss of
memory had had on him. Though she'd
been the one lying unconscious in
hospital, she hadn't been the only one
affected by what had happened.

She glanced at Nick, noting the lines

of strain etched around his eyes, and she guiltily remembered how he'd sat by her bedside for two nights.

Wanting to remain at the hospital was selfish as well as unproductive, and Dr. Jacobson seemed confident that once she was home the chances of her memory returning would be greater.

Nick was her husband, and it was entirely possible she was mistaken in thinking that their marriage wasn't a happy one. The fact that he hadn't hugged her or kissed her could simply mean he wasn't a demonstrative man.

And it wasn't unreasonable to think that finding himself in a situation where his wife no longer recognized him — had in fact forgotten she was married to him — would be difficult to adjust to or deal with.

Fate had dealt them each a challenging hand and instinctively she sensed that she wasn't the kind of person who turned her back on any situation. She wasn't a quitter, she was sure of it. She was a fighter, and she would just have to put aside her fears and misgivings for the time being and try to get on with her life.

Squaring her shoulders, she drew a steadying breath. 'Perhaps we could pick Sara up on our way home,' she suggested evenly.

At her words Nick's head snapped around in surprise and as their glances collided, she saw a glimmer of admiration and something more dance briefly in the depths of his eyes. Alison felt her heart stumble as she held his gaze.

'Are you sure?' he asked, tension still evident on his face.

'I'm sure,' she replied without hesitation.

Nick's features visibly relaxed. 'Thank you. It will mean a lot to Sara,' he said with heartfelt sincerity before turning and crossing to the door. He stopped in the open doorway for a moment and Alison thought he was going to say more, but instead he just smiled, an action that effectively brought her senses to quivering life.

When the door closed behind him, Alison stood staring at the spot where Nick had been standing. All he'd done was smile at her, and yet her whole body seemed to be reacting. Her blood was singing through her veins, leaving a warm, tingling feeling in its wake, and an ache that somehow seemed familiar tugged insistently at her insides.

It was several minutes later before she managed to drag her thoughts away from Nick and the rather devastating effect he had on her.

★　★　★

She found everything she needed in a small overnight case in the locker. Fifteen minutes later she was dressed in a pair of gray slacks and a bright blue pullover sweater.

Each item of clothing, from the cream silk bikinis and matching bra etched with exquisite lace to the slacks and sweater, fit perfectly. But as she dressed she couldn't help feeling that they didn't belong to her, that they belonged to someone else entirely.

Clothes were said to reveal a great deal about the person wearing them, but these particular pieces offered no real clue as to who she really was. The garments appeared to be new and were of a very high quality and undoubtedly expensive, making her feel awkward and ill at ease.

The overnight bag also held a few toiletries: soap, a hairbrush, toothpaste and a toothbrush. But there were no personal items such as a purse or wallet that might furnish any further hints about herself.

With a sigh she began to fold the velour dressing gown that felt so familiar to her. Closing her eyes, she hugged the robe to her much like a child would hug a favorite blanket or stuffed toy.

'Ready?' At the sound of Nick's deep voice her eyes flew open.

'I think so,' she managed to say as she began to tuck the robe into the bag, giving herself a few precious seconds before she turned to face him.

'Got everything?' He came toward her, pushing a wheelchair.

'Yes,' she acknowledged, noting with a leap of her pulse that he'd changed out of his hospital greens and back into the navy slacks and blazer he'd been wearing earlier.

Her pulse picked up speed in a reaction that was fast becoming commonplace as well as disconcerting, and not for the first time she found herself wishing she could control her response to him.

'Hospital rules dictate that you must be taken by wheelchair down to the lobby,' he told her. 'Hop on.'

Alison did as she was bid, silently telling herself that the reason her legs felt as weak as a newborn kitten's had nothing to do with Nick's presence and everything to do with the fact that she was tired and a little nervous about meeting Sara.

But moments later she was unprepared for the jolt of awareness that sprinted through her when Nick reached across to place the overnight bag onto her lap. The action brought his body in contact with hers for the space of three heart-stopping seconds.

Heat shimmied through her with an intensity that made her gasp, but to her relief the sound was lost in the noise made by the wheelchair as Nick withdrew and began to push her toward the door.

Alison's fingers curled convulsively around the handle of the bag as she fought to regain command of emotions gone disturbingly awry.

'All set?' The question came from Nurse Lucas, who'd appeared at the door.

'Yes, thank you, Nurse Lucas,' Nick replied as he pushed the chair into the hallway.

'Goodbye, Mrs. Montgomery,' Nurse Lucas said. 'Oh . . . and good luck.'

'Goodbye,' Alison murmured over her shoulder as Nick headed for the bank of elevators.

When the elevator doors opened there was barely enough room for them inside, and as a result they made the descent in silence. By the time they reached the hospital's entranceway, Alison's doubts about going home with Nick were already beginning to resurface.

'It's chilly outside,' Nick said as he brought the wheelchair to a halt. He lifted the bag from her lap. 'Your coat's in the back seat of the car. If you wait here I'll drive the car around to the front door and bring it in for you.'

'Okay,' Alison replied, glad to have a few minutes respite. Throughout the elevator ride she'd been trying to think rationally about her reaction to Nick.

She kept reminding herself that he was her husband and the fact that she'd experienced such a strong physical reaction to his touch was easily explained. No doubt he'd made love to her numerous times during their marriage.

As this thought registered, a shiver

chased along her nerve endings, inflaming her senses and sending a rush of heat through her. Her feelings for him must run deep, she reasoned. Why else would just the thought of Nick making love to her evoke this kind of heady response?

But who was the red-haired woman? The question dropped into her mind like a paratrooper into a war zone. Had Nick been having an affair? Had he been unfaithful? Could that be the reason for the tension she could feel hovering between them whenever he was near?

5

Alison bit down on the inner softness of her mouth in an attempt to distract her thoughts from the direction they'd suddenly taken.

The notion that perhaps Nick was having an affair was pure conjecture on her part, she told herself calmly. Other than the brief memory flash there was nothing on which to base the suspicion, and from what she'd seen of this man who was her husband, she found it hard to believe he would betray a trust.

Glancing beyond the sliding glass doors, she saw the subject of her thoughts striding purposefully toward the building, a coat over his arm. With a concentrated effort, she pushed aside her negative assumptions and stood up out of the wheelchair as he approached.

Not for the first time since she'd

awakened in the hospital and been told that he was her husband, was she struck by the impact of his startling good looks. But handsome didn't begin to describe the aura of power or depth of intelligence that seemed to emanate from him.

'Here we are.' Nick held out the coat for her.

'Thank you,' she mumbled, and, careful to avoid any contact with him, slid her arms into the sleeves of the woolen coat.

As they walked toward the automatic doors Alison was conscious all the while of Nick's hand at her elbow. She was relieved when he released her to open the passenger door of the gray Mercedes.

Sinking gratefully into the leather bucket seat, she reached behind her for the seat-belt strap, an action that was completely automatic, telling her quite clearly that she'd done the same thing many times before.

Her glance flew to meet Nick's, but he was carefully closing the door before making his way around the car to the driver's seat.

Alison remained silent while Nick started the engine and put the car into gear. As he pulled away from the curb Alison contented herself in simply gazing out at the passing scenery.

'How far do we have to go?' she asked, wanting to break the silence.

'Not too far,' Nick replied. 'I — We — live about a ten-minute drive from the hospital.'

'Bayview appears to be a rather picturesque town,' she commented, admiring the row of cedar trees lining the center of the boulevard that ran parallel to the hospital.

Nick flashed her a glance. 'Anything look familiar?' he asked casually.

'No,' she said, wishing she could give an answer in the affirmative.

'Did you talk to Sara? Does she know you're bringing me . . . home?' She stumbled over the word, still having difficulty getting used to the situation.

'Actually, no.' Nick responded.

Alison threw him a startled glance.

'I talked to Katie's mother,' Nick explained. 'She was just getting ready to take the kids for a drive. She was taking them to Brannigan's farm. She'd promised them they could pick out their own pumpkin.'

'Then it must be Halloween soon,' Alison said, realizing she wasn't aware of the exact time of year. But then she'd had too many other things on her mind.

'Not until the weekend,' Nick said. 'I thought Sara might be disappointed if she missed out on the trip to the farm, so I asked Jackie to give me a call when they got back. I'll pop over and pick her up then,' he went on. 'It gives you the opportunity to settle in a little first . . . before Sara gets home.'

And maybe remember something. Though Nick hadn't spoken the words aloud, she sensed he was thinking them. A shiver of anticipation skimmed through her but she said nothing, faintly relieved that the upcoming reunion with Sara had been delayed, at least for a short while.

Closing her eyes for a moment she tried without success to conjure up an image of their house . . . their home. But no picture came.

Nick was silent for the remainder of the drive. Five minutes later, he slowed the car to execute a left-hand turn into a driveway. Alison instantly recognized the wrought-iron gates — the gates she'd seen in her memory flash.

Alison's heart began to hammer painfully inside her breast as Nick completed the turn that took them through the gates. The driveway curved to the right and as the house came into view, Alison's attention was immediately captured by the gorgeous three-story Tudor-style home.

She turned to Nick as he brought the car to a halt. 'This is where we live?'

'This is where we live,' he confirmed as he shut off the car's engine.

'It's beautiful!' Her voice was slightly breathless.

Nick's mouth curved into an enigmatic smile as he leaned back in his seat and stared at the house. 'My father had this house built for my mother,' he said in a peculiar tone. 'He thought that giving her a beautiful new home to look after would keep her so busy she wouldn't notice his frequent absences.'

He paused before continuing. 'It didn't work, of course. Three months later, the day after my fifth birthday, as a matter of fact, she left and never came back.'

Alison heard the almost undetectable remnants of pain and sorrow in his voice and her heart went out to him.

'I'm so sorry,' she said softly, sincerely.

Nick glanced sideways at her, a look of surprise on his face. 'Don't be.' His reply was gruff, almost as if he regretted his momentary lapse. Reaching for the door handle, he stepped out onto the paved driveway.

Alison watched as Nick came around the car to open the passenger door.

From the moment he'd made the turn into the driveway she'd been aware of a tension growing within her at the prospect of what lay ahead.

Strangely, Nick's brief but telling tale had effectively dispelled her own fears and doubts and all she could think about was Nick as a small boy, enduring the pain of his mother's abandonment.

Had she known about his mother's desertion before? she wondered as she released her seat belt. Somehow she doubted it.

'Hey! I hope you're not looking upset on my account,' Nick said as he opened the door and offered his hand. 'I don't even know what brought that memory to mind,' he added with cool nonchalance.

The moment Nick's fingers curled around hers, Alison was aware of a tingle shooting up her arm, and as she stepped out of the car to stand beside him, it was not without some effort that she lifted her gaze to meet his.

Her breath caught in her throat when she discovered his face only inches away from hers. His strong dynamic features seemed etched out of granite and as her eyes met his, the air between them crackled with tension. His dark fathomless eyes held hers captive for a long moment and she could feel the faint yet tender caress of his breath against her cheek and smell the clean masculine scent of him as it slowly enveloped her.

A quiver of need sprinted through her, startling her in its intensity, and an emotion, quickly masked, flickered briefly in the depths of Nick's eyes.

'Perhaps this is as good a time as any . . . ' His words barely registered before his mouth came down unerringly on hers.

Shock ricocheted through her as his lips, gentle at first, quickly increased their pressure. She felt his arm move around her back to pull her body firmly against his in an action that sent her blood thundering through her veins.

Her mouth opened — from surprise

or pleasure she wasn't entirely sure — allowing his tongue free rein to explore and arouse. And as the kiss deepened it seemed to take on a life of its own, igniting a dizzying heat deep within her even as it sent erotic messages to her brain.

Abruptly as it began, the kiss was over.

'Welcome home, darling,' Nick said in a throaty whisper as he drew away.

Alison blinked and tried to corral her scattered senses. For her the kiss had been far more than a welcome home, but gazing at Nick she saw that he appeared totally in control, unaffected by what had just taken place.

'Thank you,' she managed to say, wondering at the feeling of disappointment rippling through her as he released his hold on her and moved to open the trunk of the car.

Tucking her trembling hands into the pockets of her coat, Alison turned toward the house and drew several deep steadying breaths. A cool breeze tugged at her hair, but even as she tried to force herself to study the house and her new surroundings, she was still reeling from the kiss they'd just shared.

That Nick had kissed her seemed so at odds with the quiet concern he'd shown her at the hospital. Perhaps the fact that he was a member of the hospital staff, with a reputation to maintain, was the reason for his rather cool detachment during her stay.

But there had been nothing remotely detached about the kiss he'd just bestowed on her and she was at a loss to understand the dramatic change.

'Let's get in out of the cold.' Nick's voice startled her as he came up behind her.

Alison nodded in agreement and they crossed to the front door. He unlocked it and held the door open for her, allowing her to pass into the tiled foyer. Directly in front of her lay a carpeted stairway leading majestically to the second floor.

She held her breath as she slowly let

her gaze travel around the entranceway, silently hoping for a break-through. But even as her brain acknowledged the beauty of the antique furniture scattered about, ranging from a beautiful armoire to a stunning ornate oak coatrack, the door to her memory remained firmly closed.

A feeling of disappointment washed over her as she released the breath she'd been holding. A quick glance at Nick told her that he, too, had been watching and waiting expectantly.

The smile he gave her was warm. 'Give it time,' he said softly, and the low timbre of his voice seemed somehow to reassure her. 'Let me take your coat.' He set the overnight bag on a Duncan Phyfe table nearby.

Alison slid off the coat and handed it to Nick. Turning from him she studied the scene once more. While nothing seemed familiar, there was a warmth and sense of peace radiating from the house that reached out and gently soothed her.

'First we must pay a visit to my father,' Nick said as he came to a halt beside her.

'Your father?' she repeated in a surprised voice.

'He has a small suite of rooms on the main floor,' Nick explained. 'He's bedridden and has been since he suffered a heart attack a year ago. Janet Sangster looks after him. She's his live-in nurse.'

'How old is your father?' Alison asked as Nick ushered her down the hall toward the rear of the house.

'Seventy-seven,' he replied, stopping in front of an ornate oak door. 'I should warn you, his mind is a bit fuzzy and he tends to get mixed up with the past and the present,' he added. Turning away, he knocked on the door and without waiting for an answer, he entered.

The room was a small sitting room decorated in pale pinks and greens. A heavyset woman of about fifty rose from one of the easy chairs, a book in her hand. 'Hello, Doctor. Why Alison

. . . Mrs. Montgomery, what a lovely surprise. I was so pleased to hear that you're none the worse for your accident. I'm sorry I didn't get up to the hospital to visit. How are you?' she asked with a friendly smile.

'Hello . . . ah . . . Mrs. Sangster,' Alison said, immediately liking the woman and her smile. 'I'm just fine, thank you.'

'It's so nice to have you home,' Mrs. Sangster said. 'It's been so quiet around here without you and Miss Sara. Is she with you?' she asked.

'No, Sara's still at her friend's,' Nick replied. 'I'll be picking her up in a little while. We just popped in to see Roger for a few minutes. Is he awake?'

'I'll check and see,' Janet replied. 'He was asking me about the two of you this morning.' Setting her book on the end table, she crossed to the door at the other side of the room.

'Janet is wonderful with Roger,' Nick said. 'I don't know what we'd do without her.'

The door opened and Janet reappeared. 'He's awake. In you go.' She ushered them through the door.

'Hello, Father,' Nick said as he crossed to the bed. 'We popped in to see how you are today.' He beckoned to Alison to come closer.

'Who's with you?' Roger Montgomery's voice was low and gruff, like the roar of a tired old bear.

'It's Alison.' Nick took her hand in his and gently pulled her toward him.

'Hello . . . Roger,' Alison said, trying to ignore the tingle of warmth scampering up her arm. She felt decidedly awkward and more than a little distracted at being so close to Nick.

Alison managed to smile at Nick's father, noticing instantly Nick's strong resemblance to the man lying in the bed. Yet the older man's pallid features and lined skin spoke of age and illness.

'Where's Sara? Didn't you bring the child with you?' Roger asked brusquely as he peered at her through narrowed eyes.

'Well . . . no.' She glanced at Nick for support, and he squeezed her hand.

'Sara's at her friend's, today, Dad,' Nick said. 'We'll bring her in to see you later.'

'Who did you say you were?' Roger asked, his eyes still on Alison.

Nick sighed and flashed her an apologetic glance. 'Don't be upset, this happens all the time. His memory plays tricks on him,' he said softly before turning to his father once more. 'Dad, this is Alison . . . she's my wife, remember?'

Alison's heart skipped a beat at his choice of words.

Roger smiled at her. 'Of course I remember,' he said indignantly. 'Who could forget such a pretty girl?'

'Thank you,' Alison said, feeling her face grow warm with embarrassment.

The door opened behind them and Janet Sangster reappeared. 'Sorry to intrude,' she said, 'but there's a telephone call for you, Doctor, a Mrs. Wells.'

'That's Katie's mother,' Nick said. 'I'll be right back.' Releasing her hand, he followed Janet from the room.

Alison felt a quiver of panic dance through her. She wished Nick hadn't left her alone with his father.

'Did you bring Sara with you today?' Roger's question broke the silence, catching Alison off guard. The tone of his voice was completely different, giving her the distinct impression he did indeed know who she was.

'No . . . she's at her friend's,' Alison said, repeating what Nick had already told him.

'The two of you haven't been to see me for a couple of days,' Roger continued. 'Sara's not sick is she?' he asked.

'No, she's fine,' Alison replied, guessing that Nick hadn't told his father about her accident or, for that matter, her stay in the hospital.

She cast a harried glance around the room, hoping Nick would return before Roger asked a question she couldn't answer.

But Roger had already closed his eyes and she detected a change in his breathing, leading her to think that he'd drifted off to sleep. Slowly she began to retreat toward the door. She'd only taken two steps, however, when Roger blinked and opened his eyes to stare directly at her.

'Pamela? Is that you?' he asked.

'No . . . it's Alison,' she told him, but already his eyelids had flickered shut.

To her relief the door behind her opened and Nick appeared. He glanced at his father, then motioned Alison from the room.

'I'm sorry about that,' he said as they left his father's suite and headed toward the foyer. 'That was Jackie, Katie's mother. They're back and I told her I'd be right over to collect Sara. Do you want to come with me or would you rather wait here?' he asked as he came to a halt in the entranceway.

Alison hesitated for a moment. She was beginning to feel a little over-whelmed, and the encounter with

Nick's father had been strange, to say the least.

'Actually I'm a little tired,' she told him. 'I think I'll wait here, if you don't mind.'

Nick's expression immediately changed to one of concern. 'Stay, by all means,' he said. 'Look, I'm sorry,' he hurried on. 'This must be very awkward and uncomfortable for you. I shouldn't have taken you to see my father, but as Janet said, he gets a little agitated at times and he's been asking about you every day,' Nick explained. 'Would you like to go upstairs and lie down for a while?'

'No, really. I don't need to lie down. I'll be fine.' Alison felt her pulse take a leap in silent alarm. It suddenly struck her that as Nick's wife she'd be sharing a room with him, at least under normal circumstances. But these weren't normal circumstances and she wasn't at all sure it was a situation she was ready to face.

'Why don't you wait in the den?'

Nick suggested as he crossed to the wooden double doors to the right of the front door.

He opened them and Alison moved past him and into the spacious room. One wall was completely covered with bookshelves and in front of it sat an enormous oak desk with papers, files and magazines strewn haphazardly across it. Nearby, in front of a gas fireplace, was a black leather couch with two matching chairs.

The fireplace, framed by a gleaming oak mantel, stood against the outer wall, its flame flickering a welcome. The room was warm and inviting and as she scanned the decor she was aware of Nick's steady gaze trained on her, watching . . . waiting.

But while the cosy ambience of the den seemed vaguely familiar, no memory stirred in the dark portals of her mind.

She turned to Nick. 'You'd better go. Sara will be wondering what's happened to you.'

He opened his mouth to say something, but Alison forestalled him. 'I'll be fine, don't worry,' she assured him, suddenly longing to be alone.

Nick hesitated, but only for a moment. 'I'll be back in fifteen or twenty minutes,' he said, and with that he retreated, closing the door behind him.

Alison crossed the carpeted floor to stand in front of the fire, eager for the warmth it provided. She stood for several minutes, gazing at the bluish flame licking at the artificial logs, until she heard the sound of a car engine revving up, followed by tires on the driveway outside.

She released a small sigh, relieved to be alone, at least for a little while. She had hoped that returning to this house — the house she'd been running away from — would have prodded loose some of the memories locked inside her head. But while she felt a sense of familiarity about the house, she was no nearer to uncovering the past.

Tears of frustration stung her eyes and she blinked them away, angry at herself for indulging in self-pity. She was alive and well, and judging by what Nick had told her about the accident, she'd also been incredibly lucky.

Restlessly now, she began to walk around the room, coming to a halt in front of the bay window that overlooked what during the summer months must undoubtedly be a colorful flower garden.

The flower beds were empty and the only greenery was the rhododendron and azalea bushes sitting in silent repose waiting patiently for spring to return.

The realization that she actually recognized the plants made little impact and Alison turned from the window and began to pace the room.

She stopped in front of the bookshelves and plucked a leather-bound volume from the nearest shelf. The title — *A Tale of Two Cities* by Charles Dickens — jumped out at her and instantly she recalled the powerful story. She knew she'd read and enjoyed the novel — somewhere, sometime — but where? And when?

Hugging the book against her breast, she resumed pacing, her footsteps muffled by the plush carpeting.

Nick had been gone less than five minutes, and suddenly the idea of exploring the rooms on the upper floor on her own, without his watchful gaze, had her heading for the door.

Stepping out into the foyer, she quickly closed the door behind her. The house was quiet, but her heart was thumping noisily against her breastbone as she crossed to the stairs and slowly began to make her ascent.

At the top of the stairs she instinctively turned to the right, coming to a halt at the first door, drawn by a force she found impossible to ignore. Would she find the answers she was desperately looking for behind this door?

The handle turned easily and as the

door swung open she held her breath in heightened anticipation.

The room was exquisitely decorated in shades of blue and pale green. The bedspread covering the double bed was a mass of irises, and the draperies hanging from either side of the window matched the bedspread perfectly.

The moment she stepped into the room, Alison was instantly aware of a feeling of safety . . . of comfort . . . of coming home. She crossed to the window seat with its blue and green cushions. Sitting down, she was immediately overwhelmed with a strong conviction that she'd sat here in this spot numerous times. But what exactly did it mean? It was obvious at a glance that this was a woman's bedroom and not the master bedroom as she'd expected. Indeed there was no evidence, visually at least, that the room was occupied by more than one person.

Alison let her glance slide past the beautiful walnut night tables on either side of the bed to the matching dresser beyond. A hairbrush, comb and mirror set sat on the dresser, as well as a beautiful blue-and-white porcelain figurine, but they told her nothing. She continued to scan the room, coming to a halt at the mirrored doors of what she assumed was the closet.

Would she find items of clothing in the closet? And if she did, could she assume they were hers? Surely she would recognize her own belongings!

Her head was beginning to pound now as she rose and crossed to the mirrored doors. She opened the closet door and stood staring at the variety of blouses, pants and skirts hanging inside.

Tentatively she reached out to touch a beautiful cream silk blouse, hoping that by doing so she might unlock a memory, but while everything appeared to be in the size she wore, the familiarity she'd felt when she'd put on the housecoat didn't materialize.

Frustration tugged sharply at her insides, making her want to cry out in protest, but she quelled the impulse, swallowing the angry words hovering on her lips. Taking a deep steadying breath, she bent her head for a moment in an attempt to regroup.

It was then that she noticed the suitcase lying open on the floor of the closet. Curious, she crouched down and pulled the suitcase out onto the carpet, noticing instantly that it was already packed with items of clothing.

The pain in Alison's head began to intensify. A quick check through the suitcase revealed underwear, blouses, a skirt and pants, a silk dress, stockings and shoes, all in the exact same size as the items hanging above her.

What did it mean? She sat back on her heels as a number of possibilities flooded into her head. Had she and Nick had a fight? This wasn't the master bedroom, of that she was sure. Had she moved out of the room she shared with her husband and into this one?

Why? What had happened between

them? The suitcase beside her was packed and ready to go. Did that mean she'd been planning to leave Nick? Was that what she'd been attempting to do when the accident occurred?

6

'Alison? Are you upstairs?'

Nick's voice, accompanied by the sound of his footsteps on the carpeted stairs, brought Alison instantly out of her reverie. Nick was back . . . with Sara!

Alison quickly wiped away the tears tracing a path down her cheeks, tears she hadn't even been aware of until now, and guiltily she pushed the suitcase back into the closet.

Jumping to her feet, she shut the mirrored doors and stepped out into the hallway seconds before Nick appeared at the top of the stairs.

'Here you are,' Nick said when he saw her, and there was more than a hint of relief in his tone.

Alison managed to smile, hoping Nick couldn't hear the thundering of her heart as it beat a frantic tattoo against her breast. 'I was looking for the bathroom,' she said, keeping her tone even.

Nick held her gaze, his eyes boring into hers as if he was somehow trying to see inside her very soul.

'Uncle Nick! Uncle Nick, did you find her?' This time the voice belonged to a child and Alison's nerves jangled in apprehension as she tore her gaze from Nick's and allowed it to rest on the tiny blond-haired figure running up the stairs toward them.

'Sara!' Alison breathed the name on a sigh as a feeling of love washed over her.

'Ally! Ally!' Sara said as she scurried past Nick and threw herself at Alison.

Alison swiftly bent to catch the small bundle of energy, lifting her into her arms in an action that somehow seemed totally familiar. Sara's grasp was tight around Alison's neck and suddenly she was fighting back fresh tears as she returned the child's hug.

Overwhelmed by the show of affection, the uninhibited outpouring of love, Alison felt her throat close over with emotion.

'Hey! Take it easy!' Nick cautioned Sara, but there was more than a hint of laughter in the low rumble of his voice.

Through the blur of tears, Alison glanced at Nick, seeing the look of love on his face as he in turn gazed at the child. A pain, sharp and unexpected, tore through Alison, catching her off guard, and she closed her eyes, burying her face in Sara's sweet-smelling hair until she once again felt in control.

'I missed you,' Sara said as she slowly released her hold.

'I missed you, too,' Alison replied sincerely, sensing that the child needed to hear the words.

'Are you really okay?' Sara's blue eyes stared anxiously into Alison's. 'Uncle Nick says you've losted your memory, that you don't remember anything,' Sara continued, a worried frown on her face.

'Unfortunately Nick is right,' Alison replied, keeping her tone light, not wanting to frighten Sara.

'But you remember me, don't you?' Sara asked, her gaze intent, her eyes wide.

Alison smiled. 'Indeed I do,' she replied. And while her words were not strictly true, neither were they a lie. During a brief memory flash she had seen and recognized Sara, and there seemed little point in upsetting the child by telling her that was all she remembered, especially when Sara was still so obviously in need of reassurance.

Sara twisted around to look at Nick. 'See, I told you Ally wouldn't forget me.'

'And you were right,' Nick replied smoothly as he threw Alison a grateful glance.

'I'm so glad you're home.' Sara sighed as she hugged Alison once more.

'Me, too,' Alison said, surprised to discover that she actually meant it. Whatever had happened between her and Nick had had nothing to do with the child. In fact Alison felt a strong attachment to Sara and instinctively sensed that their relationship was a very special one.

'Does your head hurt?' Sara wanted to know.

'A little. But it's getting better,' Alison said, warmed by Sara's touching concern. 'I hear you went to a farm to pick out a pumpkin today,' Alison continued, wanting to direct the conversation away from herself.

Sara nodded vigorously. 'Katie's mom took us. Want to see the pumpkin I picked out?' she asked eagerly.

Alison smiled. 'I'd love to.'

'It's the biggest pumpkin in the whole world,' Sara told her enthusiastically.

'Hey, be careful,' Nick cautioned. 'You'll fall if you don't stop wriggling.' Reaching over, he lifted Sara from Alison's arms, setting her down on the carpet.

Sara immediately put her hand in

Alison's, staring up at her with an expression of love and adoration. Startled, Alison threw a glance at Nick, in time to see an indecipherable emotion flash in the depths of his eyes.

'Let's go check out that pumpkin, shall we?' Nick stood aside and motioned Alison and Sara down the stairs.

The pumpkin was indeed a large one, and Nick was given the dubious honor of carrying it to the kitchen.

'Can we carve it now?' Sara asked, her blue eyes sparkling with excitement.

Alison saw the hesitation on Nick's face. 'Halloween is still a few days away,' he said, and at his words Sara's happy expression immediately began to fade. 'But I suppose there wouldn't be any harm in carving it now,' Nick hurried on. 'What do you think?' He addressed the question to Alison.

'I think we could carve it now,' Alison responded, finding it difficult to ignore the look of entreaty on Sara's face.

'We'll need to cover the table with something,' Nick said, obviously getting

116

into the spirit. 'Sara, you know where all the old newspapers for recycling are kept.'

Sara nodded and scampered away, returning in a matter of seconds with an armful of newspapers. Together they spread them out on the kitchen table. Nick set the pumpkin on top.

'We have to draw a face on it first,' Sara instructed as she crossed to the row of drawers next to the sink.

Nick met Alison's gaze. 'Listen, we can do this later. Sara will understand if you're tired . . . ' His words were no more than a whisper, offering her the chance to back out if she chose to take it.

'No . . . I'm fine,' she assured him, shying away from being alone, sure that she would only spend the time thinking about the suitcase she'd found upstairs and puzzling over what it might mean. For a moment she was tempted to ask Nick about it, but she curbed the impulse. Now was not the time or the place.

'Here's a felt pen.' Sara held up the object, then closed the drawer and returned to the table.

Nick lifted Sara onto a chair. 'While you two decide what kind of face Mr. Pumpkin should have, I'll start making dinner,' he said. 'How does spaghetti sound?'

'You know pasghetti's my favorite.' Sara flashed Nick a smile as she leaned toward the pumpkin, the felt pen held tightly in her hand.

'That's fine with me,' Alison replied, managing to hide her surprise at the fact that this man who was her husband appeared to be quite at home in the kitchen.

The hour that followed was, for Alison, one of the happiest since waking up in the hospital. Sara was a warm, loving, intelligent little girl who chattered on about her friend Katie and the play-school they attended together.

After Nick cut the opening on the top of the pumpkin, Alison helped Sara scoop out the seeds and clean out the inside. As they worked at their separate tasks, Alison was aware of a strong sense of peace and harmony.

Again she was struck by the notion that she'd done this before, that she'd spent time with Nick and Sara. She felt completely at home with them, and the positive feelings and congenial atmosphere led her to believe that the three of them enjoyed a good relationship — not unlike that of a real family.

'Time to clean up and set the table. Dinner's almost ready,' Nick informed them, cutting into Alison's thoughts as she put the finishing touches to Mr. Pumpkin's grinning face.

'Where shall we put Mr. Pumpkin?' Alison asked.

'The end of the counter is fine,' Nick replied.

Sara helped Alison lift the pumpkin off the table and onto the counter.

'Look, Uncle Nick! Mr. Pumpkin's grinning at you.' Sara giggled.

Alison smiled to herself as she

returned to the table and began to fold up the newspapers they'd spread out earlier. Suddenly a headline on the top left-hand corner of one of the pages caught her attention and she focused in on the short item.

Honeymoon Postponed for Local Doctor and His New Bride.

Dr. Nicholas Montgomery, Surgeon and Assistant Administrator of Bayview Hospital, was married this afternoon to Miss Alison Beaumont of Seattle, Washington. Their plans for a honeymoon had to be postponed, however, when his new bride was taken to hospital after an accident outside the couples' home.

Alison felt as if she'd just been hit by a speeding train. The blood drained from her face and it was all she could do to hold back the cry of astonishment that threatened to erupt from somewhere deep inside.

It had to be a mistake, she told herself calmly as her mind refused to accept the implications of what she'd just read. She scanned the piece a second time, but nothing had changed and this time the words *honeymoon* and *new bride* seemed to jump out at her like bullets from a gun.

'I'll put the papers away if you get out the place mats,' Sara said, but Alison couldn't have responded if her life depended on it.

Head pounding, she dropped into the nearest chair, her entire body trembling as she tried to deal with the shock she'd just received.

Thankfully Sara was too preoccupied with carrying the newspapers out to notice Alison's reaction.

'You'll find place mats in the second drawer.' The low rumble of Nick's voice reached her but she had no idea what he'd said.

Suddenly Nick was crouched at her feet. 'What is it? Are you all right? What happened?' He fired the questions at her in rapid succession, his voice threaded with anxiety, and Alison could feel the tension emanating from him.

A shiver of apprehension chased down her spine as she tried to speak. 'The paper . . . there was something. I just read . . . ' She stumbled over the words, finding it difficult to even think straight.

'I don't understand,' Nick said, a hint of exasperation in his tone now. 'Have you remembered something?'

'No . . . ' She lifted a hand to push her hair out of her face. 'The papers . . . on the table . . . ' she went on, but before she could say more Sara came running into the kitchen.

Alison glanced over Nick's shoulder in time to see Sara brake to a sudden halt, obviously sensing that something was wrong. A look of distress appeared on the child's face.

Nick muttered under his breath and, rising, he crossed to where Sara stood, frozen to the spot. The child's lower lip began to quiver and her blue eyes filled with tears.

'Hey, sweetheart, don't. There's nothing to cry about.' Nick swooped down and gently lifted Sara into his arms.

Sara sniffed and kept her gaze on Alison. 'You're not going away again, are you?' Sara asked in a shaky voice.

Alison blinked in surprise. 'No . . . no, of course not,' she replied, anxious to reassure the child.

Getting to her feet, Alison instinctively moved to within inches of Nick, and Sara instantly reached out to her. Alison braced herself for the child's weight and lifted Sara into her arms.

'You promised that after you and Uncle Nick got married you'd stay with us for always,' Sara said timidly.

Alison felt her pulse leap at the words and her eyes flew to Nick's in time to see an emotion flicker briefly in his dark eyes before it was quickly controlled. Feeling as if he'd just closed a door on her, shutting her out, Alison suddenly found herself fighting back tears of anger and frustration.

'No one's going anywhere.' Nick's tone was cool, calm and collected. 'I think we should all sit down and have supper. It's been a trying day, for everyone.'

Alison heard the plea for compliance in his voice and she responded. 'Your Uncle Nick is right.' Alison eased Sara away from her. 'I don't know about you, but I'm starving and that spaghetti smells wonderful, doesn't it?' She smiled encouragingly at the child.

Sara managed a weak smile before glancing at Nick, as if to confirm that all was back to normal once again.

Alison lowered the child to the floor and it wasn't long before they were all seated at the table. Though there were awkward silences throughout the meal, Alison did her best to keep the conversation going, asking Sara questions about play-school and what she'd been learning.

Sara's answers were short and uninspiring, making Alison aware of the fact that the harmony and peace they'd enjoyed earlier had been replaced by a thin veil of tension.

The food was delicious, but Alison found it difficult to concentrate, her thoughts continually returning to the item she'd read in the newspaper. Alison Beaumont was the name she'd been identified with and while she knew it must be her name, it meant nothing to her.

And overriding all the other questions spinning around inside her head was the realization that the day of the accident had also been the day she'd married Nick.

How could she have forgotten one of the most important days of her life — her wedding day? She realized, with quiet desperation, that she was silently praying for another memory flash . . . anything that would shed some light, however small, on the past, on the memories still locked securely inside her head.

Suddenly the shrill sound of the telephone echoed through the kitchen and with a mumbled apology Nick rose to answer its summons.

His conversation was brief and when he replaced the receiver, Alison could tell from his expression that whoever had called had not been the bearer of good news.

'I was hoping this wouldn't happen, at least not tonight,' he said as he returned to the table. 'But unfortunately these things are never predictable.'

'What's wrong?' Alison asked.

'It's one of my patients. I have to go back to the hospital.' There was a hint of sadness in his tone that tugged at her heart.

'Don't worry. Sara and I will be fine,' Alison said, sensing that his reluctance to leave possibly stemmed from this being her first night home from the hospital.

'I'll help load the dishwasher,' Sara announced proudly.

'Thanks, Sara.' Nick smiled at his

niece, then glanced over at Alison once more. 'I don't know how long this will take . . . '

'Take all the time you need,' Alison said, finding it strange that she should want to reassure him.

'Ally will put me to bed and read me a story like she always does. Right?' Sara said, gazing up at Alison.

'Right,' Alison echoed with a smile. Putting Sara to bed wouldn't be a problem, in fact she was sure she'd enjoy the task, and judging by Sara's comment, she'd obviously done it many times before.

Alison glanced at Nick and her breath fluttered to a halt at the look she could see in his eyes. She had the impression he wanted to say something, something important, but after a brief hesitation all he said was, 'I'll be back as soon as I can.'

With Nick's departure the tension that had been so evident throughout the meal dissipated. As promised, Sara helped Alison load the dishwasher, and after tidying the kitchen it wasn't long before the little girl started to yawn.

'Someone's ready for bed, I think,' Alison teased, only just managing to stifle a yawn of her own.

Sara led the way upstairs and on down the hall to her bedroom, which was next door to the room Alison had explored earlier.

The child's room was decorated in pink and white, with one wall covered in a wallpaper adorned with jungle animals. The bed itself was practically hidden beneath a layer of stuffed animals, and the shelf under the window overflowed with books of all kinds.

But while Alison felt a strong sense of familiarity about the room, she was somewhat disappointed that it stirred no memories.

Half an hour later Sara finally hopped between the sheets and Alison sat beside her on the bed to read a story.

By the time the story ended Sara was

having trouble staying awake, but when Alison quietly slipped off the bed and bent to kiss the child's cheek, Sara's eyes instantly flew open.

'Don't go . . . please!' she pleaded in a sleepy voice, her hand curling around Alison's and clutching it tightly, tugging her back onto the bed.

'I'll stay right here until you're asleep, I promise,' Alison said softly, settling back down on the bed. Sara smiled and fought to keep her eyes open. Less than a minute later Sara's eyelids drifted shut, her breathing slowed and her fingers relaxed their hold on Alison's as she fell into a deep sleep.

Alison waited several minutes more before getting up and tiptoeing from the room. She left the bedroom door open just a crack and made her way to the room next door.

Crossing to the window seat, Alison sat down on the cushions and, kicking off her shoes, brought her feet onto the seat beside her.

Leaning against the edge of the window frame, she gazed out at the night sky. The stars were obscured by dark clouds and as the silence of the evening wrapped around her, Alison felt some of the tension of the long and emotion-filled day gradually drain away.

A feeling of well-being stole over her and instinctively she sensed that it was solely connected with the room she was in. She felt safe and protected there. With a sigh, she closed her eyes.

But her moment of peace was short-lived as the questions that had leapt into her mind when she'd read the newspaper item earlier came bubbling to the surface once more, refusing this time to be put off or ignored and reminding her of the startling revelation that the day of the accident had also been the day of her wedding to Nick.

Why had she been running from the grounds? Where had she been going? The fact that her marriage to Nick had been but a few hours old shed a new light on the situation and at least offered an explanation for the presence of the suitcase she'd found packed and ready for use.

They'd planned to go on a honey-moon . . . the newspaper had reported as much. Abruptly she brought her thoughts to a halt. She wasn't sure she was ready to pursue that subject, at any rate there had been no honeymoon. Something had happened in the interim. It was the only explanation that made sense. What had it been?

Hugging her knees, Alison began to rock gently back and forth, trying without success to explore the dark caverns of her mind in search of the answers.

But there were no answers, only more questions. Had she been running away from Nick? Had he given her a reason to be afraid?

No, Alison shook her head in instant denial, immediately dismissing the notion. Whatever she felt for Nick, and she most definitely had feelings for him, fear was nowhere on the list.

Why? Why? Why? The question played inside her head like a broken record.

Though she was convinced she had nothing to fear from Nick, she was equally sure that her relationship with him was somehow the crux of the matter. And once again she found herself thinking about the memory flash of seeing Nick in another woman's arms.

Alison drew a deep steadying breath, trying to relax. Slowly she allowed her thoughts to drift back to the moment when Nick had appeared in her hospital room, a few minutes after she'd recovered consciousness.

He hadn't acted like her husband then. But perhaps that hadn't been altogether his fault. She'd been confused and disoriented and when he'd appeared on the scene, dressed in a white coat, she'd simply assumed he was just a doctor.

She remembered the look of relief she'd glimpsed on his handsome features — as well as one of caution — when she'd confessed to him that she couldn't remember anything.

He'd naturally slid into the role of doctor and no doubt had he told her then that *he* was her husband, he might well have traumatized her more than she had been already.

When she *had* learned that he was her husband, she'd quickly jumped to the conclusion that the reason for his less than loverlike behavior toward her, and the tension that seemed to crackle between them, was because they had been experiencing problems . . . marital problems.

She'd been wrong about that. Could she be wrong about everything? Alison dropped her head onto her knees for a moment and inhaled deeply. She was totally confused about Nick . . . about everything . . .

She moaned softly, partly due to frustration and partly due to the fact that the pain inside her head had become a full-blown headache.

A knock at the bedroom door brought her instantly alert and she glanced up to see Nick standing in the doorway. Her breath caught in her throat at the sight of him.

'I wondered if I might find you here,' he said with more than a hint of weariness in the low timbre of his voice.

Alison swung her feet off the window seat and stood up feeling strangely on the defensive. 'This is my room, isn't it?' At her question, Nick's dark eyes registered shock as they darted to meet hers.

'Yes, this is your room.' With quick strides he closed the gap between them. His hands came up to grasp her upper arms. 'You've remembered. Your memory has come back, hasn't it?'

It was all she could do to meet his gaze as she tried without success to ignore the tingling heat spreading through her. The air between them was alive with tension and Alison was aware of his rich masculine scent invading her senses, sending her thoughts spinning chaotically.

She shook her head. 'No . . . I

haven't remembered anything,' she told him, angry at herself for not being able to control her body's reaction to him. 'This room just feels familiar, that's all,' she explained a little breathlessly.

Nick released her and studied her face for a long moment. 'Something's happened,' he persisted. His eyes bored into hers. 'What about in the kitchen earlier? What was that all about?'

Alison drew a ragged breath and sidestepped Nick, moving to stand at the foot of the bed, simply wanting to put some distance between them. 'I saw something in the paper,' she told him wearily.

'The newspaper? I don't — ' Nick broke off, his expression swiftly changing. 'What did you see?' he asked with obvious annoyance.

Alison bristled at his tone. Suddenly she was angry — angry at being in the dark, angry at not knowing — and tired of it all.

'Why didn't you tell me the accident happened on our wedding day?' she demanded. 'What difference would it have made?' She drew a fortifying breath. 'And what was I doing out in the middle of the street? Why was I running away?'

A look of stunned surprise flashed in the depths of Nick's eyes at her question.

'I wish I knew,' Nick said with a tired sigh. 'I wish I knew.'

7

Alison stared at Nick in disbelief. Of all the answers she might have expected, this wasn't one of them.

'You don't know?' she said, her tone incredulous.

Nick cursed under his breath. 'That's right,' he replied tersely. 'I have no idea where you were going or what you were doing out in the street that afternoon.'

Alison was silent for several long seconds, pondering his words. 'That doesn't make any sense,' she said, almost to herself. 'Something must have happened.'

'Not to my knowledge.' Nick's comment cut through her thoughts bringing her attention back to him and to the rigid set of his jaw.

Alison deliberately met his gaze, wanting to see his reaction to the question she was about to put to him. 'Did we have a fight?' she asked abruptly.

She was only guessing of course, but suddenly she found herself wondering if the tension shimmering between them was an indication of a highly charged relationship.

Nick held her gaze for a long moment. 'No, we didn't have a fight.' His dark eyes gave nothing away. He ran a hand through his hair and sighed. 'I doubt it will make any difference now if I tell you that we'd come upstairs after the ceremony to change and get ready to leave.' He paused. 'You wanted to finish packing, but when I came to get your suitcase, to put it in the car, you weren't here.' He came to a halt and this time he was the one watching for a reaction.

'That's when Janet came running upstairs to tell me there'd been an accident outside . . . ' he continued after a brief hesitation. 'You could have bowled me over with a feather when I found you lying on the road out there.'

Alison heard the emotion in Nick's voice, reminding her once more that she wasn't the only one affected by the accident or her memory loss. 'I'm sorry,' she said, instantly feeling contrite. 'I keep forgetting that this can't be easy for you, either.'

'Easy?' Nick repeated in a startled whisper. 'No, it hasn't been easy. And it isn't over yet,' he added. 'Not for either of us.'

Alison didn't respond, she was busy focusing her thoughts on Nick's brief description of the events prior to the accident. He'd said she'd been packing, and that confirmed her earlier conclusion. They'd been preparing to leave, on their honeymoon, no doubt, though Nick hadn't said as much.

Honeymoon! Suddenly the word conjured up all kinds of tantalizing images, sending a shiver of awareness chasing through her.

Closing her eyes, Alison deliberately pushed these thoughts aside, concentrating instead on trying to wedge open the door to the past, to those forgotten moments just before she ran out into the street.

Perhaps she'd seen or heard something outside and gone to investigate? But surely if that had been the case she would have summoned Nick.

Something must have happened! Something that had sent her running from the house and out into the street without a thought to anyone. Her behavior seemed to point to an emotional reaction. But what or who had been the cause of it?

'Hey, we're both exhausted. I think that's enough for one day, don't you?' Nick spoke softly and Alison felt his hands gently clasp her shoulders once more.

This time his touch set off a bevy of tiny explosions somewhere deep inside. An unfamiliar tingling sensation danced across her nerve endings, arousing a hunger that had nothing to do with food. Alison drew a quivering breath, an action that only succeeded in filling her head with his heady masculine scent.

A strange intoxicating heat was spreading through her, stirring her senses and making her legs feel unusually weak.

She glanced up at the face only inches from her own, her gaze drawn inexorably to his mouth.

He was going to kiss her she thought with alarming clarity, and she felt her muscles tighten in anxious anticipation. And he had every right to kiss her, a small voice inside her head reminded her. After all, he was her husband.

'No!' The word burst forth from her in urgent denial and she wrenched herself free from his arms. Heart pounding, she glanced up into those dark impervious eyes in time to see a look of pain and sorrow glitter in their depths, a look he quickly controlled.

'I'm sorry,' he said in a tight voice. 'I wasn't about to seduce you if that's what you were thinking.'

Alison felt her cheeks grow hot at his words. She knew she was overreacting, and she couldn't really blame him for being angry with her. But the realization had hit her like a bolt from the blue that, as her husband, Nick had a legal right to take her to his bed . . . to make love to her.

And suddenly it was all too much. She was utterly exhausted and totally confused and until she could sort out the mess she was in — a mess that included finding herself married to a man as devastatingly attractive as Nick Montgomery — she needed time and space and understanding.

'I'm sorry,' she mumbled, wishing with all her heart that she could somehow magically turn the clock back and resolve the mystery hovering over them like storm clouds on a sunny day.

'You don't have to apologize,' Nick responded. 'You've been through quite an ordeal these past forty-eight hours,' he said evenly. 'What we both need is a good night's sleep. I'll see you in the morning.' With that he turned and left the room, closing the door behind him.

Alison stood for several minutes, staring after him, surprised to discover that now that she was alone, she felt lost and more than a little lonely. With a sigh she turned and crossed to the dresser, easily locating a nightdress in one of the drawers.

In the bedroom's adjoining bathroom she prepared for bed and as she slid between the sheets she tried not to think about Nick, or about what might have happened if he'd kissed her.

★   ★   ★

Alison stretched and rolled over, smiling to herself in her sleep. She was dreaming. Dreaming that she was walking across a carpeted room toward Nick, who looked stunningly handsome in a dark suit with a white shirt and black bow tie. He was standing in front of an oak fireplace, watching her, a hint of a smile on his face.

On either side of the fireplace stood two beautiful flower arrangements made up of red, pink and white carnations. Soft music played in the background and she was aware of several people standing nearby.

Ahead of her she noticed Sara,

wearing a pretty pink dress and holding a small basket of flowers. The atmosphere in the room was joyful, and glancing down she was somewhat surprised to see that she was carrying a bouquet of carnations the exact color of the ones on display.

A wedding! She was at a wedding. She loved weddings. As she drew level with Nick she glanced over her shoulder, hoping for a glimpse of the bride, but there was no one behind her.

Frowning now, she turned to see an elderly man with a smiling face wearing a clerical outfit, directly in front of her. She felt her pulse quicken in alarm and glancing down at her attire for the first time, she noticed she was wearing a beautiful two-piece white suit made of exquisite silk and trimmed with lace.

Alison's eyes flew open and she sat up with a start, her heart drumming a frantic tattoo against her breast. A quick glance around the bedroom somehow reassured her, and as her pulse slowed to normal she realized that her dream had been a memory flash . . . a flash of her wedding to Nick . . . she was sure of it.

Another small piece of the past had resurfaced, or at least enough to convince her that her marriage to Nick had indeed taken place. She brought her knees up to her chin and put her arms around them.

She was making progress — she had to believe it. But she quickly reminded herself that she still had a long way to go and, until she recovered her memory completely, the question of why she'd been running away would remain like a thorn in her side, effectively frustrating her at every turn.

A knock at the bedroom door brought her out of her reverie. But before she could speak or move, the door opened to reveal Nick, dressed in gray slacks and a bloodred sweater, carrying a breakfast tray. At the sight of him looking so relaxed yet dynamic, her heart skipped a beat.

'Ah . . . good . . . you're awake! I was

beginning to think you were going to sleep all day,' Nick said, a hint of amusement in his voice.

'What time is it?' Alison asked as she made a frantic but unsuccessful grab for the bed sheet.

'It's almost eleven.' Nick leaned over to set the tray across her knees.

'Eleven!' Alison repeated in a shocked tone. 'But it can't be.'

'I'm afraid it is,' Nick told her. 'You slept well, I hope?' he asked as his ebony eyes met hers.

Alison swallowed convulsively and felt her face grow hot with embarrassment. 'Yes . . . I did,' she managed to say, realizing with a start that the scooped neckline of her nightdress afforded him a view of her breasts. 'Ah . . . thank you.' She dropped her gaze to the tray, noticing immediately the tiny bud vase holding a single red rose.

'How's your head today?' Nick's tone was businesslike.

Instinctively her hand moved to touch the back of her head. 'It feels fine,' she told him.

'Let me take a look,' he said, and before she had time to form a refusal she felt his hands gently brush her hair aside with a touch that was heart-stoppingly seductive.

He bent toward her for a closer look and Alison's breath caught in her throat as she was assaulted by the smell of lemons and soap as well as an earthy scent that was undeniably male.

'Hmm . . . Yes, that's healing nicely,' Nick commented as he drew back.

Alison slowly released the breath she'd been holding, praying silently Nick wouldn't notice that her nipples were erect and aching with need.

She crossed her arms in front of her. 'Does that mean I can wash my hair?' she asked, a faint tremor in her voice.

'I don't see why not,' Nick replied.

'Oh, and thank you for break-fast . . . ' she said, keeping her eyes averted, wishing he would leave.

'No problem,' he said. 'Actually I had

an ulterior motive in bringing you break-fast.'

Alison threw him a startled glance. 'You did?' What on earth did he mean? she wondered, unable to control the warmth spreading through her body in response to his comment and the smile she could see curling at his mouth.

'Sara wanted to wake you this morning, but I told her you needed to rest,' Nick explained. 'However, I did promise that I'd bring you with me when I pick her up after play-school.'

'Oh . . . I see.' Alison wasn't sure whether she should be relieved or disappointed. 'When does school get out?' she asked.

'At noon,' he told her.

'Oh . . . then I'd better get a move on.' Unfolding her arms, she reached for the glass of orange juice on the tray.

'I'll be downstairs in the den, when you're ready,' Nick told her, and with that he turned and left the room.

★ ★ ★

Alison was surprised how hungry she felt and it didn't take her long to devour the bowl of hot cereal and the banana muffin Nick had brought her.

The coffee was hot and strong and as she took a sip her gaze shifted, as it had numerous times during the past ten minutes, to the red rose sitting in the tiny bud vase. Its delicate fragrance teased her nostrils and tugged at her heartstrings.

A red rose generally signified romance and love. Was Nick trying to send a message? With a sigh she set the tray aside and headed for the bathroom.

As the hot spray of the shower washed over her she found her mind filled with thoughts of Nick. She still couldn't believe he was her husband — that she was married to a man so strong and dynamic, so devastatingly handsome.

A shudder ran through her as she recalled the way her body had responded to his nearness. That she found him attractive was obvious, telling her clearly that her feelings for him ran deep . . . why else would she have married him?

But her instincts were also informing her that she shouldn't make rash assumptions or decisions about their relationship — that until her memory returned she should take things slow and easy, and not let her heart overrule her head.

She was encouraged by the fact that the flashbacks she'd experienced so far had been significant, had revealed something important. That is, all except the one where Nick had been holding a beautiful redheaded woman in his arms. Unlike the one in which she'd seen and remembered Sara, Alison had no idea who the woman was, or how she fit into the scheme of things.

Twenty minutes later Alison closed the bedroom door and made her way downstairs. From the clothes hanging in the closet, she'd chosen a pair of camel slacks, a long-sleeved silk blouse the color of sand and a matching cardigan.

She'd washed her hair and brushed it out with care, tying it loosely at the nape of her neck with a multicolored scarf. While she'd stood contemplating what to wear, she'd noticed a garment bag hanging at the rear of the closet and on closer inspection she'd recognized the white silk suit — the one she'd worn on her wedding day.

Now Alison came to a halt outside the door to the den and, taking a deep breath, she knocked lightly, then entered. Nick glanced up from the papers strewn over the oak desk and as she met his gaze she saw a glimmer of appreciation dance in the depth of his eyes.

'You look lovely.' His compliment sent a shiver of awareness chasing through her.

'Thank you,' she replied, wishing she could control the blush that warmed her cheeks.

'All set?' He rose from the chair and lifted a navy sports jacket from the back of his chair.

'Yes . . . but I was wondering . . . '

she began hesitantly. 'Shouldn't you be at the hospital? I mean — I realize the accident must have caused a few problems for you, but I hope what happened hasn't interfered with your work . . . ' Her voice trailed off as she watched the ripple of Nick's muscles as he slipped his arms into the sleeves of his jacket.

'Don't concern yourself,' he assured her. 'We'd only planned a brief . . . ah . . . honeymoon . . . just the weekend,' he explained. 'And barring emergencies, I'd already arranged to take this week off so that we could spend some time with Sara.'

Alison felt her pulse hiccup at the mention of their honeymoon. She moistened lips that were dry. 'Oh . . . I see,' she said, touched by his obvious concern and consideration for the child.

'It's a little chilly out, today. You'll need a coat.' Nick had moved past her to hold the door open.

Alison nodded as she walked ahead of Nick into the foyer. Crossing to the closet near the front door, he extracted a lovely camel wool coat and held it for her.

She was careful to avoid contact with him and in a matter of minutes they were walking together toward the Mercedes.

Nick held open the car door for her and as she lowered herself into the passenger seat, she found her thoughts lingering on his comment about their honeymoon.

A faint tremor rippled through her as Nick took his seat behind the wheel and she tried without success to turn her thoughts away from him and back to the problem of her memory loss.

Only when her mind was occupied elsewhere was she able to forget that this incredibly sexy, disturbingly handsome man was her husband. But the tension that shimmered between them was a constant reminder, telling a story all its own and leaving Alison to wonder if Nick was aware of the affect he had on her.

Her thoughts shifted back to the previous evening, to those moments in her bedroom when she'd thought Nick was going to kiss her. She knew with every fiber of her being that had he kissed her, she wouldn't have had the strength or the inclination to deny him anything.

But even as she acknowledged the power he seemed to have over her, she sensed that Nick wasn't the kind of man who would simply take what he wanted without regard for her feelings.

Alison glanced at Nick, who was intent on the task of making a left turn. She studied his profile, noting the strong set of his jaw, giving the impression that it had been chiseled out of a piece of granite. His nose was straight and aristocratic, and his eyebrows were as black as night, hooding ebony eyes that gave nothing away and added more than a hint of mystery to the man.

His hair was thick and black and inclined to curl, and suddenly her fingers itched to feel its silky texture.

And his lips . . . surely the kiss he'd

bestowed on her yesterday to welcome her home hadn't been the first kiss they'd shared, she reasoned. But how could she have forgotten the pure magic of his mouth igniting such heat, eliciting a response from somewhere deep inside her?

Alison felt her heart contract as a need that was fast becoming familiar began to spread through her. Not without some effort, she dragged her gaze back to the road ahead just as Nick completed the turn and brought the car to a halt in the parking lot of a single-story building.

'I'll be right back.' Releasing his seat belt, he climbed from the car and closed the door.

Glad of the chance to regroup, Alison watched as Nick's long stride took him across the parking lot and toward the door of the building. Three other cars pulled into the lot, but though Alison smiled and acknowledged several friendly waves, she didn't recognize or remember anyone.

It was not without some relief that, a few moments later, she saw Nick reappear with Sara at his side. Alison saw the anxious expression on the child's face and watched as Nick took Sara's hand and pointed to the car.

Sara's face broke into a wide smile and she began to wave at Alison as they made their way toward her.

'I told you she was waiting in the car,' Nick said as he opened the rear door and ushered Sara inside.

'Hi, Sara.' Alison twisted around in her seat and smiled a welcome. 'How was school today?'

'Fine,' came the quick reply. 'Did you really sleep in?' Sara asked as Nick snapped the child's seat belt into place.

'I'm afraid I did,' Alison replied.

Nick closed the back door and returned to his seat behind the wheel.

'But you've never slept in before,' Sara told her. 'You're not sick . . . you won't have to go back to the hospital, will you?' The anxiety was there in her voice again.

'No, I'm feeling much better,' Alison assured her as Nick carefully eased his way out of the parking lot and back into the stream of traffic. 'I was just tired, that's all.'

'Oh.' Sara obviously wanted to believe her, but Alison could see from the look in the little girl's blue eyes that she was still concerned and Alison found herself wishing she could take Sara in her arms and reassure her with a hug.

'Why don't we drive out to Greystone Cove and have a picnic in the car?' Nick asked in a cheerful voice. 'I made up a few sandwiches for us and brought some fruit for dessert.'

Sara's attention was instantly diverted. 'A picnic in the car? Really? Can we, Uncle Nick?' she asked excitedly.

'As long as Alison feels up to it.' Nick flashed Alison a quick glance.

'Sound's like a wonderful idea,' Alison replied, wondering if Greystone Cove was a place they'd visited before. But it wasn't difficult to see that Nick was trying to distract Sara by suggesting an outing and she couldn't help admiring his tactic.

★ ★ ★

Greystone Cove was indeed an apt description for the picturesque inlet and sandy beach Alison found herself on half an hour later. The journey out of Bayview and along the tree-lined coast road was in itself enjoyable and when Nick brought the car to a halt in the paved parking lot overlooking the beach, the sun peeked tentatively from behind a cluster of clouds, warming the temperature several degrees and raising her spirits along with it.

They sat in the car and ate the sandwiches and fruit Nick had prepared, watching the waves building until they crashed noisily onto the shore.

'Can we go for a walk now?' Sara asked as soon as she finished eating.

'Of course,' Nick replied, and immediately Sara scrambled out of the car and ran around to the passenger side, eager for Alison to join her.

Nick locked the car doors and together they made their way toward the path that led down to the sand. The beach was deserted and as the wind tugged playfully at Sara's blond curls, she laughed aloud and smiled up at Alison.

Waves splashed onto the sand, and up above a group of sea gulls squawked as if they were scolding them for daring to intrude on this their private domain.

'Race you two to the rocks,' Nick challenged in a teasing tone, pointing to the group of gray stones sticking out of the sand about fifty yards along the beach.

Sara squealed in delight. 'Come on, Ally,' Sara urged before she scampered off across the beach.

Alison threw a fleeting glance at Nick and saw him grinning at her, poised and ready to run.

Her breath caught in her throat in response to his irresistible grin. 'Last one there is a rotten egg,' Alison tossed the challenge back at him, and without waiting for a reply, broke into a run.

Alison had no intention of catching up with Sara, whose little legs were eating up the yards, but for some perverse reason she wanted to beat Nick.

The wind buffeted her, stealing her breath away and making her cheeks tingle. She felt the scarf she had tied around her hair earlier being snatched away by the breeze, but she didn't stop.

Sara reached the rocks first, climbing haphazardly onto a small group sticking out of the sand. Alison could hear Nick's footsteps pounding on the sand behind her and out of the corner of her eye she saw that he was coming abreast of her.

Suddenly her foot came down on something half buried in the ground and before she knew what was happening, she toppled over, face first, onto the sand.

The air was knocked from her lungs and she lay still, stunned but unhurt, for several seconds.

'Alison! Dear God! Are you all right?' Nick's voice, urgent and charged with fear, reached her. She rolled over onto her back to find him kneeling on the sand beside her, a worried look on his handsome features.

She felt her heart tilt in response to the concern she could see on his face and strangely the urge to comfort and reassure him was her first thought.

She smiled up at him. 'I'm fine. Really I am.' There was a breathless quality to her voice that had nothing to do with her fall and everything to do with the dark-eyed man looming over her.

Nick held her gaze for what seemed like an eternity, and she watched in fascination as a flame flickered to life in the depths of his eyes before it vanished, leaving her to wonder if perhaps she'd been mistaken.

'Ally! Ally!' Sara shouted as she came running toward them.

Nick quickly hopped to his feet, pulling Alison with him, then releasing her almost immediately.

'I'm okay.' Alison turned to give Sara a reassuring smile, all the while painfully aware of the man beside her.

Would he have kissed her had they been alone? she wondered. Would he have whispered words of love? How *did* Nick feel about her?

A mere moment ago, when she'd seen the flash of desire in his eyes, she was almost convinced that his feelings for her ran strong and deep. But looking at him now, his expression unreadable, Nick seemed to have withdrawn to somewhere private and out of reach.

Those forgotten moments, that space in time when she'd run from Nick on their wedding day, appeared to have created a wall of mistrust between them. And unless her memory returned, she wasn't at all sure their marriage would survive.

8

'Perhaps this wasn't such a good idea, after all,' Nick said a few moments later.

'Nonsense,' Alison replied. 'I tripped, that's all. Sara, let's see if we can find a pretty shell to take home with us,' she continued, determined not to let her fall spoil the outing for the child.

'I saw some pretty shells over by the rocks,' Sara said tentatively.

'Show me.' Brushing sand from her coat, Alison followed Sara to the rocks.

For the next fifteen minutes Alison and Sara clambered over the clump of gray rocks in search of shells. Nick chose not to join in their explorations. Instead he wandered a little farther along the beach and stood staring out across the water, his gaze intent on the horizon beyond.

Alison found herself glancing his way

now and then, wishing she could somehow ease the strained look evident on his face.

The sun slid behind the clouds and soon the chilly breeze from the water began to penetrate the layers of their clothing.

Sara, dressed in pants and a warm ski jacket, was too busy enjoying herself to notice that the temperature had dropped. But Alison saw the telltale slash of pink on the child's cheeks, and when she touched Sara's hands, she wasn't surprised to discover that they were cold.

'I think we've got enough, now.' Alison took the pieces of broken clam shell Sara held out to her.

'Time to go. It's cooling off.' The comment came from Nick, whose approach neither Sara nor Alison had heard. 'Let's head back to the car.'

Alison nodded.

'Can we make some hot chocolate when we get home?' Sara asked.

'I think that can be arranged,' Nick

replied, the hint of a smile curving at the corners of his mouth.

Alison purposefully avoided Nick's gaze as she put the pieces of shell Sara had handed her into the pocket of her coat. Then, taking Sara's hand, they began to walk toward the path leading to the parking lot.

Nick fell into step beside them, taking hold of Sara's free hand. Suddenly he lifted the child off her feet, swinging her gently between them.

The sound of Sara's laughter rang out over the small sheltered cove and, unable to resist, Alison laughed, too. She threw a quick glance at Nick and felt her stomach lurch at the sight of his answering smile.

With his hair windswept and in riotous disorder, he'd never looked more appealing, and the chill she'd been experiencing moments before seemed to melt away under the warmth of his smile.

'More! More!' Sara yelled, effectively drawing Alison's attention away from

Nick. Together they swung Sara into the air, bringing her down to earth when they reached the car.

The shelter of the car was a welcome respite from the chilly temperatures outside. Nick quickly started the engine and before too long the heater was blowing hot air at them.

Sara snuggled into the corner of the back seat, and almost before they reached the coast road her eyelids began to droop.

'She's asleep,' Alison said a little while later as she glanced over her shoulder. 'Isn't it amazing how quickly children fall asleep.'

'I know some adults who have a knack for it, too,' Nick commented, a hint of amusement in his tone.

They drove in silence for a while. 'Tell me about Sara,' Alison asked, suddenly filled with a need to know the circumstances that had brought the child into Nick's life.

Nick tensed at her words, his knuckles turning white as he tightened his hold on the steering wheel. He drove for several minutes without speaking and Alison was beginning to think he was going to ignore her request.

'Sara's father was my older brother, Richard — ' He broke off as a car pulled out to overtake them. 'Richard and his wife, Nadine, were killed in a car accident a year and a half ago,' Nick continued, and Alison heard the pain etched in his voice as he spoke.

'I'm sorry,' she said softly, fighting the impulse to put her hand on his.

'He was forty-six when he died,' Nick continued. 'Forty-six years old . . . ' He lapsed into silence, a silence Alison did not disrupt. That he was still dealing with the loss of his brother and sister-in-law was apparent and she regretted that she'd been responsible for reminding him of the tragedy.

'Sara wasn't with them when the accident happened.' Nick's voice cut through the hum of the car's engine. 'They were driving to the baby-sitter's to pick her up when some teenagers who were hot-rodding on a side road lost control of their car and ran into them head-on.'

Nick's voice was controlled and void of emotion, but Alison sensed the anger and frustration just below the surface.

'I was appointed Sara's legal guardian.' Nick resumed his story. 'And so she came to stay with us in Bayview. My father was in reasonably good health then, but Richard's death affected him deeply.'

And you, too, thought Alison, seeing the lines of sorrow on his face. Instinctively she put her hand on his arm in a gesture that was meant to comfort.

Nick threw her a startled glance, his eyes dark and unreadable, and Alison immediately withdrew her hand, wishing now she hadn't brought up the subject.

'I'm sorry. I didn't mean to upset you,' she said, trying to ignore the way her pulse had sped up when she touched him. 'You've done a wonderful job with Sara. She's lucky to have you, and her grandfather,' Alison said sincerely.

'Thank you.' Nick glanced briefly in her direction. 'But if you want to know the truth,' he continued, 'you're the one who deserves the credit.'

'Me?' Alison stared in shocked silence at Nick. 'I don't understand.'

'When Sara came to stay with us, she was shy and very quiet . . . too quiet. She'd withdrawn from the world. And who could blame her? She'd lost the two most important people in her life. We could hardly get a word out of her,' Nick went on. 'But somehow you were able to break down the barriers she'd erected. That's one of the reasons she's so attached to you.'

Though a warm glow had spread through Alison at his words, she only wished she could remember for herself the role she'd played in Sara's recovery.

That Sara must have been distraught with grief over the death of her parents had undoubtedly been the cause of her withdrawal, but Alison found herself wondering when and how she'd come into the picture. Before she could put a voice to the question, however, Nick pulled into the driveway leading to the house.

'Wake up, pumpkin. We're home,' said Nick as he brought the car to a halt.

'Have you still got my shells?' Sara asked in a drowsy tone.

'Yes. They're in my pocket,' Alison said.

'Come on sleepyhead, I'll carry you inside.' Nick climbed from the car and opened the rear door. 'Alison, would you unlock the front door?' he added, tossing her the keys.

Alison deftly caught the keys and, climbing from the car, quickly crossed to the front door. Nick joined her a few moments later with Sara in his arms.

'Can I go and show Gramps my shells?' Sara asked when Nick set her down.

'Good idea,' Nick said. 'I'll make

some hot chocolate while you two pay him a visit.'

Alison retrieved the handful of shells from her coat pocket and handed them to Sara. 'I'll make the hot chocolate,' she offered, thinking Nick might also like to visit his father.

'I'm quite capable, thank you,' Nick said.

'I didn't mean . . . ' Alison began, feeling her face grow warm. She turned from hanging her coat in the closet in time to see the twinkle of amusement in Nick's eyes.

'Just teasing,' he said. 'I'm sure my father would much rather have two beautiful women pay him a visit.' Nick went on.

'Come on, Ally,' Sara urged, all signs of her sleepiness gone.

Alison followed Sara to her grandfather's rooms, thinking all the while of Nick's comment. Did he really think she was beautiful? Janet greeted them warmly, saying Roger was awake and in good spirits.

Clutching her shells tightly in her hands, Sara headed into Roger's bedroom with Alison bringing up the rear.

'Well, hello,' Roger said brightly. 'How nice to see you both.'

'Hi, Gramps. Look what I have,' Sara said as she crossed to the bed holding out her hands to show him the shells.

Alison moved to the foot of the bed and Roger glanced at her and smiled. 'So what have you two been up to?' he asked.

'We went for a drive to Greystone Cove,' Alison told him, pleased that he appeared to remember her today and was indeed in good spirits.

'That's where we found the shells,' Sara said.

'They're very pretty,' Roger dutifully assured her. 'Didn't you go to school this morning?' he asked.

'Yes,' Sara said. 'Miss Matthews, my teacher, read us a story and then we had to draw a picture. I drew a picture of my pumpkin,' Sara told him proudly. 'It's almost Halloween, you know.'

'Halloween? Is it really?' Roger's expression was rather vague and uncomprehending.

'We're having a party at school on Friday and on Saturday it's my friend, Katie's, birthday and she's having a sleep-over party. Everyone's going to dress up for that, too,' Sara recounted excitedly.

'My goodness, two parties sound like fun. And what are you dressing up as?' he asked.

'Alison's making a ballerina costume for me,' Sara informed him before turning to Alison for confirmation.

'A ballerina costume?' Alison repeated in a startled tone. 'I mean . . . that's right, a ballerina costume,' she quickly amended with a smile, making a mental note to ask Nick, at the first opportunity, about the costume and where it might be. That Sara assumed Alison hadn't forgotten about the costume was obvious. She had to have been working on it prior to the accident.

'It will be ready for Halloween, won't

it?' Sara asked, a hint of anxiety in her voice.

'Absolutely,' Alison replied, vowing silently that no matter what, Sara's costume would indeed be ready in time for Halloween.

'I don't mean to interrupt.' Janet appeared in the doorway. 'But I was asked to tell you that the hot chocolate is ready.'

'Oh boy!' Sara flashed Alison a grin.

'Will you come and see me again soon?' Roger's tone was wistful.

'Of course,' Alison promised as she followed Sara from the room.

Sara scampered ahead into the kitchen and was already sitting at the table, sipping hot chocolate and counting the shells spread out in front of her when Alison entered.

Nick stood at the sink, washing his hands. He'd discarded the navy jacket and bulky red sweater he'd worn earlier and at the sight of the muscles rippling beneath his pale blue shirt, Alison felt a jolt to her senses as her pulse picked up speed.

'It's there on the counter,' Nick said as he glanced over his shoulder at her.

'Thanks,' Alison murmured, wondering if she'd ever get used to her reaction to this man. As she reached for the mug, the telephone sitting nearby rang, startling her.

'Would you get that?' Nick asked.

Alison hesitated for a moment before picking up the receiver. 'Hello.'

'May I speak to Nick, please?' Alison felt the hair at the back of her neck stand up at the sound of the woman's voice. The breathless tone, the cadence — there was something familiar . . . For a fleeting second a memory danced on the edge of Alison's mind, drifting just out of reach before she could grasp it.

'What . . . ? I'm sorry. May I ask who's calling?' Alison was suddenly aware of a chill sprinting down her spine and she held her breath, waiting for the woman to answer.

'This is Pamela Jennings. Is Nick there?' This time the woman's tone was edged with impatience, and the faint hope that hearing the voice again might help corral the memory, faded and died.

'Uh . . . yes. He is,' Alison responded. 'Just a moment, please.' She turned to Nick. 'Pamela Jennings,' she said, relieved that her voice at least gave away none of the turmoil going on inside her.

'Thank you.' Nick quickly dried his hands before taking the receiver from her.

'Hello, Pamela,' Nick said. His greeting was followed by a long silence, during which he listened attentively.

Alison frowned as she picked up the mug of hot chocolate and came around the counter, pondering all the while on the strong conviction that not only did the woman's voice seem familiar, but she was sure she'd heard the name somewhere, and not that long ago.

She heard Nick make several brief comments before hanging up. And glancing at him, Alison saw a thoughtful expression on his face.

'Anything wrong?' she asked, hoping he might offer an explanation and reveal something about the caller.

Nick met her gaze and slowly shook his head.

'No . . . nothing,' he said with a faint smile. 'How was my father?' he asked in an obvious attempt to change the subject.

'Much brighter today,' Alison responded, her curiosity aroused more than ever now. She wished she could recall where and when she'd heard the woman's name before.

'Gramps liked my shells,' Sara said, joining in the conversation.

'That's nice,' Nick commented, but Alison saw that he still seemed preoccupied.

'Alison says she's going to finish my ballerina costume in time for Halloween,' Sara went on.

Nick's head came up with a start and he met Alison's gaze with an intensity she found disconcerting. She could read the silent question 'you remembered?' in his eyes.

She moved her head in a negative motion and for a moment she wasn't sure whether Nick looked relieved or disappointed.

It wasn't until the evening meal was over that Alison was afforded an opportunity to talk to Nick alone. Sara had jumped down from the table and scooted upstairs to her room to retrieve a book she'd talked about several times during the meal, a book she seemed to think belonged to Alison.

'Now that Sara isn't here, I wanted to ask about the Halloween costume I'm supposed to be making,' Alison said as soon as the little girl was gone.

'There's a small bedroom upstairs at the end of the hall,' Nick told her. 'You turned it into a sewing room of sorts when you started work on the costume,' he explained.

'I think I'd better take a look and see what's left to be done to the costume,' she said. 'I wouldn't want Sara to be without one on Halloween. And she also said something about Katie's birthday party.'

Nick smacked his forehead with the heel of his hand. 'That's right . . . I'd forgotten all about that,' he said with a sigh. 'And it's on Saturday. Damn. And that's not all that's slipped my mind lately,' he muttered almost to himself.

'What do you mean?' Alison asked.

Nick ran his hand through his hair in a gesture of frustration. 'That's the same night as the masquerade ball the hospital's putting on. It's part of their fund-raising campaign this year,' he explained.

'And . . . ' she prompted, unsure just what he was getting at.

'It's just that as a member of the hospital board — ' He broke off.

' — you're expected to attend,' Alison finished for him.

'That's right,' he acknowledged. 'I bought the tickets ages ago. It seemed like a good idea at the time,' he added.

'A masquerade ball,' Alison repeated. 'Don't tell me I'm making costumes for that, too?' she asked trying not to feel panicked.

Nick smiled and shook his head. 'No. Nothing like that,' he assured her. 'Actually, I believe you rented costumes for both of us — ' He stopped. 'Anyway, it's not that important and I can always put in a brief appearance, just to keep the administration happy,' he added.

Alison was silent for a long moment. It was obvious from what Nick had told her that they'd made plans to attend the ball. And while he'd assured her he could put in an appearance on his own, she sensed that he was merely being considerate.

Perhaps the ball was to have been their first appearance in the community as husband and wife. This notion was pure conjecture on her part, of course, but if her guess was indeed correct, she couldn't let Nick go alone, could she?

'Here's the book!' Sara said as she rejoined them in the kitchen.

Alison took the rather well-worn,

hardcover book from Sara's hands. The moment her fingers closed around the book Alison was immediately assailed with a strong feeling of familiarity. Glancing down at the title she saw that the book was called *Fairy Tales, Old and New.*

She flipped open the cover and noticed the childish writing on the inside page. The name *Alison Beaumont* had been printed with painstaking care across the page, and seeing it, Alison felt her heart shudder to a halt.

Images and memories of her childhood rushed like a torrent through her mind. The book was hers . . . given to her by her parents on her fifth birthday, a few months before they'd drowned in a boating accident.

The memory of the moment her aunt had told her of their deaths was so vivid that Alison had to close her eyes against the onslaught of pain she knew would accompany it. Hugging the book against her breast, Alison drew a ragged breath.

'Alison! What is it? Are you all right?' Nick's anxious voice seemed to come from somewhere faraway, but when she opened her eyes he stood directly in front of her.

'I remembered . . . ' she said in a choked voice, and at her words she saw an emotion flare in his eyes.

'Tell me!' he urged, his hands coming up to clutch her shoulders.

Over Nick's shoulder Alison suddenly glimpsed Sara's white face and tear-filled eyes. Her look of confusion and fear so mirrored the emotions churning inside Alison that her immediate thought was to reassure Sara and eliminate the fear she could see in the little girl's eyes.

'Sara, it's all right.' Alison freed herself from Nick's grasp and quickly crouched to Sara's level. 'I didn't mean to frighten you.'

'It's my fault, isn't it?' Sara's voice wavered and her tears overflowed, forging a path down her pale cheeks.

'No . . . darling, nothing is your

fault.' Alison sent a cautionary glance at Nick as he knelt beside her. 'I remembered something, that's all,' Alison went on in a soothing tone, hoping her voice would help reassure the child.

Sara took a tentative step toward Alison.

'You remembered something?' Sara repeated as she wiped her tears with the back of her hand.

'When I woke up in the hospital I couldn't remember what happened or how I got there,' Alison said carefully. 'Uncle Nick explained to you that I'd lost my memory, didn't he?' she went on, with a quick glance at Nick.

Sara nodded.

While Alison didn't want to upset the child further, she also felt that Sara needed and deserved an explanation. 'Well, my memory still hasn't completely returned, and every once in a while I see, or hear, or touch something and suddenly without warning a missing piece of my memory comes back.'

'Oh . . . and that's what happened

just now?' Sara asked with obvious interest.

'That's exactly what happened,' Alison replied. 'This storybook belongs to me. I've had it for a long time . . . ' She stopped and patted the volume clutched tightly against her chest.

'Since you were a little girl like me,' Sara quickly supplied. 'That's what you told me,' she added.

Alison nodded. 'And when you gave the book to me just now . . . ' She stopped and tried to swallow the hard nugget of emotion suddenly lodged in her throat.

'You remembered something!' Sara finished with a smile.

Alison nodded and, reaching out, took hold of Sara's hand, thinking all the while that now she understood the reason why she felt such an affinity with the child. They'd both been orphaned at a young age — they'd both lost the two people they'd cared about most in the world.

As Sara moved into the circle of

Alison's arms, a ripple of relief flowed through her and she felt the sting of tears in her eyes. Glancing at Nick she saw a glimmer of respect and admiration in the depths of his eyes.

'Can we read a story from the book, now?' Sara asked, obviously appeased by Alison's explanation.

'It's almost time for bed. How about we make that a bedtime story?' Nick suggested as he stood up.

'Aw . . . ' Sara started to protest.

'No arguments!' Nick scolded in a teasing tone as he plucked Sara off the floor and pretended to toss her into the air.

Sara started to laugh, and at the sound Alison felt her own tension gradually seep away. She'd been grateful that Nick had maintained a silence throughout her explanation, but she'd also been intensely aware of his rigid control as he crouched beside her.

It was pleasing to know that in the midst of the turmoil he, too, had had Sara's best interests at heart. But on reflection he seemed to be the kind of man who rarely put his own needs first.

He provided a comfortable home for his bedridden father when a care center would undoubtedly have been a more practical, and possibly less stressful, solution. As well, he'd taken on the added responsibility of caring for his brother's child, and that in itself was an act of love and selfishness.

'More! More!' Sara shouted, breaking into Alison's wayward thoughts.

'More . . . nothing . . . ' Nick said in a slightly breathless voice. 'It's upstairs and into bed with you, young lady,' he added, setting her on the floor.

'You said you were going to read me a story, remember?' Sara's tone was serious.

'Of course I'll read you a story,' Nick quickly assured her. 'But first I have to make a quick phone call to the hospital.'

'Come on. I'll help you get ready for bed,' Alison said, and together they made their way from the kitchen.

Ten minutes later, Sara, dressed in a warm nightie, her face washed and her teeth brushed, jumped up onto her bed and snuggled beneath the covers.

As Alison bent to tuck in the blankets Nick appeared in the doorway.

'Which story would you like me to read?' he asked as he picked up Alison's book from the dressing table.

''Sleeping Beauty',' Sara said. 'That's the one where the prince has to kiss the lady to wake her up,' she explained.

'I like that one, too,' Alison said as she bent to kiss Sara good-night.

'Aren't you going to stay and hear the story?' Sara wanted to know.

'I thought I'd see how much more there is to do on your ballerina costume,' Alison replied, thinking that with Nick's tall figure hovering over them the bedroom was already a little crowded.

He stood at the foot of the bed, his six-foot frame dominating the room. Alison's pulse was behaving erratically simply because he was there, and she wasn't sure she was up to sitting near him while he read Sara a story.

'Will my costume be ready tomorrow?' Sara asked, her eyes wide with anticipation.

'I don't know. We'll have to see.' Alison wasn't sure she'd even remember how to sew and she didn't want to disappoint Sara should the costume require a lot more work. She began to back away from the bed.

Suddenly she came to an abrupt halt as she collided with a warm solid object. She knew from the riotous response ricocheting through her, that she'd backed into Nick. And when his hands came up to steady her, she had to close her eyes for a fleeting moment as a longing so strong she could barely contain it caught her unawares.

She could feel the searing heat of his body through her clothes and she could feel the warmth of his breath against her neck as he bent toward her. Tiny explosions of sensation erupted within her in a reaction that left her feeling

188

weak and disoriented.

'Sorry!' she mumbled, breaking free of his grasp and flashing a smile at Sara as she hurried from the room.

Out in the hall, Alison came to a halt and leaned heavily against the wall, waiting for the shock wave to subside.

As the roar in her ears gradually diminished, it was replaced by the muffled tones of Nick's voice as he began to read 'Sleeping Beauty.'

In the fairy tale, the prince had awakened his love with a kiss, and Alison found herself wondering if Nick was aware that he, too, was in possession of a magic equally as powerful.

9

Alison drew a steadying breath and slowly made her way to the room at the end of the hall that Nick had mentioned earlier. As he'd explained, the room had indeed been set up as a sewing room.

A sewing machine sat on a sturdy table under the window and an iron and ironing board stood just inside the door. On top of the ironing board was a bright pink leotard, and attached to it was a skirt netting of the same shade.

Alison instantly felt a sense of familiarity with the surroundings and as she crossed to the sewing machine the feelings merely strengthened.

Lifting the pink ballerina costume from the ironing board, she quickly determined that the netting was merely pinned on to the leotard and all that remained to be done was to machine-sew it.

She sat down at the machine and automatically located the On switch. Her fingers seemed to move of their own volition as she reached for the sewing box on the floor and retrieved the spool of matching pink thread. After checking that there was thread on the bobbin, she set about readying the machine.

There was no hesitation in her movements, telling her quite clearly that she was an accomplished sewer, and soon the quiet thrum of the motor could be heard as she fed the material past the pressure foot.

The hum of the machine was somehow comforting and Alison was glad to have something to do to take her mind off those heart-stopping moments in Sara's bedroom when she'd bumped into Nick.

Each time her thoughts veered in that direction, a shiver of awareness would dance across her skin, reminding her of her body's tumultuous response to him.

She tried to tell herself that the

reason she found him dangerously attractive was only natural — after all, he was her husband! And surely in the course of events leading up to their wedding, they must have spent time together — how else could they have formed a relationship, fallen in love?

Gently easing up on the foot pedal, Alison sighed. How she wished her memory would return. Only then could she hope to get on with the rest of her life.

A tap at the door brought her head around and every nerve leaped to vibrant life when she saw Nick.

'How's the costume coming?' he asked as he crossed to stand behind her.

'Actually it's almost done,' she replied, bending her head to the machine and pretending to adjust the pressure foot, all too aware of the man standing only inches away.

'It looks great. Sara will love it,' he commented.

'Thank you. I hope so,' Alison said. 'There isn't much to it, really. Besides, I like to sew, it's been a hobby of mine for a long time,' she added, surprised that this information seemed to trip off her tongue almost of its own accord.

'You have a talent for many things,' Nick observed, his voice skimming over her like a caress and adding to the tension hovering between them.

'I brought your book,' Nick went on, placing it on the end of the ironing board. 'I thought you might like to look through it again . . . see if it jogs your memory some more.'

'Thank you.' Alison wished he would leave. This room was infinitely smaller than Sara's and she was concerned that he would tune in to the tension vibrating through her.

'I have some paperwork that needs taking care of,' Nick said. 'I'll be in the den if you need me.'

'Fine,' Alison mumbled, and closed her eyes in mute relief when he moved away.

'Oh, by the way.' Nick came to a halt in the doorway. 'There's a board meeting at the hospital tomorrow afternoon that I have to attend. Sometimes these meetings go on for hours,' he said.

'No problem. Sara and I will be fine,' Alison quickly assured him before turning her attention back to her sewing.

Pulling the tutu free of the machine, Alison picked up the scissors and began to snip the loose threads. The emotions Nick had so easily aroused were still churning inside her and as she worked she held her breath, waiting for Nick to leave.

The tingling sensation at the back of her neck warned her that he was standing in the doorway watching her, and not until she heard the door close did she release the breath she'd been holding and slump forward like a rag doll.

She listened to the sound of his footsteps retreating down the hall, and only when she could no longer hear them did the tension within her ease.

Setting the tutu aside, she rose to her feet, gently rubbing the muscles at the back of her neck.

Spotting the storybook on the ironing board Alison gently ran her fingers over the cover. When her hand closed around the well-worn volume, she felt tears prick her eyes as once again those painful childhood memories came rushing to the fore.

She had only a vague recollection of her parents, their faces long faded from her memory. After the accident that had taken their lives, she'd gone to live with her father's older sister, but other than her clothes, a few toys and the storybook, she hadn't been allowed to take anything that might be considered a keepsake.

It hadn't taken Alison long to realize that her aunt was a bitter woman, with no feelings of love or affection for the niece who'd been left in her care. And there were even times during the years that followed that her aunt made Alison feel as if *she* was somehow to blame for her parents' demise.

She learned, as well, from comments her aunt Harriet had made, that she had never approved of her brother's choice of a wife. Not until she was older had Alison ventured to ask if there were any photographs of her parents, any pictures that would help keep their memory alive for her.

There were no pictures of them, or of Alison when she was a baby. Alison had grown up in a house without joy, without laughter, without love, and she'd quickly mastered the art of keeping a low profile.

The book, clutched tightly against her breast, was the only link she had left to the two people who had loved her and wanted her.

Alison closed her eyes as feelings of relief washed over her at the realization that these memories, both precious and painful, had not been lost to her forever.

The tears she'd been struggling to contain throughout her painful walk through the past escaped from beneath her lashes and with a sob she relinquished her hold on her emotions.

She didn't hear the soft tap on the door, nor did she hear it being opened.

'Alison, I just — ' Nick broke off.

Startled at the sound of his voice, Alison spun around.

'What is it? What happened? Are you all right?' Nick came instantly to her side.

Alison bit down on the inner softness of her mouth in an effort to staunch the flow of tears, dismayed that he'd come upon her in such a state of distress.

'I'm sorry,' she whimpered.

'Damn it, don't apologize.' Nick thrust a handkerchief at her.

'Thank you.' Alison blew her nose and wiped the tears from her eyes.

'Why were you crying?' Nick asked gently, and Alison was aware of the taut lines of his body as he waited for an answer.

She swallowed. 'I was thinking about my parents, remembering,' she told him in a choked voice. 'This book was the last thing they ever gave me before they died.' She sniffed, trying with difficulty to ignore the accelerated beat of her heart, due, she knew, to Nick's nearness.

'I see,' Nick said softly. 'The book did trigger some more memories then. You've never mentioned your parents before.'

Drawn by the sympathy and understanding she could hear in his voice, Alison met his gaze. Awareness, like a bolt of lightning, crackled between them, making it impossible for her to think or breathe.

Eyes as black as night and glittering like polished ebony held hers captive for several heartrending seconds, enticing a response from somewhere deep inside her.

She felt as if she were being pulled by an invisible thread, drawn toward him like the proverbial moth to a flame, unable — and unwilling — to resist the powerful force of his attraction.

Every cell in her body seemed to be crying out to him, willing him to haul her into his arms and make her his own.

When it came, the kiss was achingly sweet and sinfully tender. The book slipped unheeded to the floor as Alison felt the blood sing through her veins, taking her on a journey of discovery as sensation after sensation reverberated through her.

Her fingers instantly found their way to his hair and she delighted in the feel of its silky texture even as the urge to get closer became an ache she couldn't seem to appease.

The clean male scent of him stormed her senses, awakening a need that left her quivering. His tongue teased and tormented until she moaned softly in sweet surrender as he pushed her closer and closer to the edge of reason.

Then suddenly, without warning, it was over. Dazed and disoriented, Alison tried to focus on the features of the man holding her at arm's length.

'No. This isn't right . . . ' Nick's voice

vibrated with tension and, jolted by what she perceived as rejection, Alison had to fight to control emotions gone dangerously awry.

Though she could see by the rapid rise and fall of Nick's chest that he was not unaffected by the kiss they'd shared, it was small consolation.

'I'm sorry.' Her voice was little more than a hoarse whisper as she broke free of his grasp.

'Damn it, Alison . . . I'm the one who should be apologizing, not you.' Nick spat out the words in an exasperated tone as his hands fell to his side. 'The timing is all wrong . . . ' he went on in a strained voice, ' . . . and besides, there are a few things we need to resolve . . . '

Alison drew a steady breath and lifted her eyes to meet his. For a fleeting moment she thought she saw a look of regret flash in the depths of his eyes, but it was gone before she could be sure.

'I came to tell you that the hospital called. I have to fill in for Dr. Matheson for a few hours,' Nick said shortly, dragging a hand through his hair in an action that shouted of both frustration and annoyance. 'He's come down with the flu virus that's doing the rounds.'

'Then you'd better go,' Alison said with a calmness she was far from feeling. She desperately needed to be alone to restore order to emotions that were in total chaos.

'I hate to leave you like this . . . ' Nick bit out the words.

'Please . . . just go . . . ' She knew that if he didn't leave in the next few seconds she would surely break down and make a complete fool of herself.

Nick took a step toward her and Alison instantly tensed, putting her hands up to ward him off. She saw his lips tighten in an angry line and noted the pulse throbbing at his jaw. Then, with a muttered oath he turned and abruptly left the room.

Alison hugged herself tightly, afraid that she might fall to pieces. Slowly she began to count to twenty. She strained to hear the sounds that would tell her Nick had left the house.

Not until she reached eighteen did she hear the front door close, followed a few seconds later by the noise of a car engine springing to life.

Picking up the forgotten book, she crossed to the window. She leaned her forehead on the cool glass and watched the red taillights of the car until they disappeared down the driveway.

Feeling much as if she'd been bruised and buffeted by a freak windstorm, Alison sank into the chair nearby.

The kiss she'd shared with Nick a few minutes ago had shaken her to the core, and even now she was still reeling from its affect.

She had wanted him with a need as primitive and old as time itself, and desire still simmered beneath the surface like a volcano before an eruption.

But the fact remained that on the day of her marriage to Nick, something had happened to drive her from the house, to make her want to run away from him and their future together. And until the door to her past was unlocked and the truth uncovered she couldn't allow herself to give in to the need he could so easily arouse.

Alison spent the night tossing and turning in a vain attempt to alleviate the ache throbbing inside her. She'd occupied the hours by trying to find answers for some of the questions buzzing inside her head.

It had occurred to her that having her own room in the house seemed somehow strange. One explanation that had come to mind was that she'd simply moved in a few days prior to their wedding. But while that seemed reasonable enough, she had the distinct impression from a number of things Nick had said, and from the feelings of familiarity she'd experienced since returning to the house, that she'd occupied the bedroom for a much longer period of time.

But overshadowing this was the

question of who exactly was Pamela Jennings? And what was her connection to Nick? Alison was positive she knew the woman — there was something about the name, and the voice, that struck a chord.

Was Pamela Jennings the woman she'd seen in the memory flash? Was she the stunningly attractive red-head Nick had been holding in his arms.

Alison tried to think rationally. Perhaps Pamela Jennings was a colleague, a doctor who worked with Nick at the hospital. That could have been where she'd heard the name before . . . at the hospital. A memory flickered like an old black-and-white movie on the edge of her mind, but hard as she tried to pull the images into focus, they kept drifting away.

Wide awake now, she glanced at the clock on her bedside table and saw that it was six-thirty. Wanting to avoid a repeat of the previous morning when Nick had unexpectedly appeared with a breakfast tray for her, Alison pushed back the covers and headed for the shower.

As the warm spray splashed over her, she made the decision to simply ask Nick a few questions, maybe even mention Pamela by name and watch for his reaction.

Dressed in black slacks and a pale pink sweater, she quietly made her way downstairs. Once in the kitchen, it only took but a few minutes to put on a pot of coffee. While the coffee was brewing, she set the place mats on the table and arranged glasses and plates, then popped two slices of bread into the toaster, all the while rehearsing what she would say to Nick.

She'd just opened the refrigerator door when she heard a noise behind her. Glancing over her shoulder, she saw Nick, wearing dark green corduroy pants and a long-sleeved green-and-white striped cotton shirt, enter the kitchen.

Her heart jumped into her throat at the sight of him and a tingling heat swept through her, making her forget everything but the man before her.

His hair, still wet from the shower, was slicked back from his face, revealing the clean, strong lines of his facial features.

'You're up early,' Nick commented as he crossed to the counter.

'Coffee's almost ready.' Alison's words came out in a hoarse whisper. She turned back to the fridge, hopelessly lost and wondering what she was looking for.

'Any orange juice?' Nick's voice came from directly behind her and she felt her pulse jump in alarm.

'Right here,' Alison replied, thankful that her tone was slightly more normal as she reached for the jug sitting on the top shelf. Closing the fridge door, she turned to find him standing directly in front of her, an empty glass in his hand.

A faint tremor ricocheted along her arm as she poured juice into his glass, but if Nick noticed her reaction he made no comment.

'Thank you.' He moved away and quickly drank down the juice.

Alison watched through lowered lashes and noted the lines of strain near his mouth. Behind her the toaster popped, and setting the jug on the counter, she reached for the bread.

'I'm glad you're up. I was going to leave you a note,' Nick said as he moved to the table to pick up a coffee cup. 'I have to go in to work today. That flu has felled another two doctors, and as a result the hospital is short-handed,' he explained.

'What about Sara?' Alison asked. 'How will she get to play-school?'

'You can drive her there,' Nick promptly replied. 'It isn't far. I'll draw you a map.'

Panic danced through Alison at his words. 'Don't you need the car? I'm not sure . . . I mean . . . '

'You can use your car,' Nick said calmly. 'It's been in the garage since last week. With all that's happened I forgot about it. You took it in for a tune-up,' he explained. 'I called McBride's Garage yesterday and someone is bringing it over this morning.'

'My car? I have a car?' Alison asked, finding this news astonishing to say the least.

'Yes,' Nick confirmed. 'And before you ask . . . yes, you have a driver's license and yes, you're a very good driver.'

'But if I have a license, where is it?' Alison asked. 'I've been wondering if I have a purse or wallet or something. But I haven't come across anything like that in my room.'

'I have it,' Nick said as he poured coffee into a cup.

'You do?' Alison couldn't hide the surprise she felt.

'You'll find it upstairs in my room. It's on the dresser,' he told her. 'It's been sitting there for a while, but I don't remember how it got there.'

'You think it's safe for me to drive?' Alison asked, thinking she'd retrieve the purse first chance she got.

'Unless you'd rather not, I can't see that it will be a problem,' Nick replied easily. 'You haven't forgotten how to drive — you've just forgotten that you can. As soon as you get behind the wheel it'll come back to you, I'm sure.'

Alison wished she had as much confidence in herself as Nick appeared to. But maybe he was right. It wasn't the thought of driving that worried her as much as not being sure exactly where she was going. But Bayview didn't appear to be a town bustling with freeways and busy streets. And if Nick drew her a map . . .

'You can always call a cab,' Nick's voice cut through her thoughts. He glanced at the gold watch on his wrist. 'I've got to go. Will you be all right?' he asked. 'I can give you Jackie's phone number, that's Katie's mom. I'm sure she wouldn't mind picking up Sara and taking her to school . . . '

'No, I'll take her,' Alison said. She met Nick's gaze and saw a flicker of admiration dance briefly in his eyes.

'Good,' Nick said. 'I'll draw that map for you.' He crossed to where the telephone sat on the counter and reached for the message pad nearby. 'I probably won't be home till late,' he said as he sketched out a series of lines. 'There's that board meeting this afternoon.' He scribbled several street names, then glanced up at her. 'Look . . . this isn't exactly fair . . . expecting you to cope with all this. If it's easier, Sara can miss school for a day or two . . .'

Alison could see the concern mixed with frustration on his face. 'Don't worry, I'll figure things out.'

Nick smiled. 'You know, you're a remarkable woman. I only wish . . .' he began, then stopped abruptly, his smile fading. 'The play-school runs from nine o'clock till noon. If you have a problem with the directions, ask Janet. I must go.' He downed the remainder of his coffee and headed for the door. 'There's a number in the book by the phone if you should need to get through to me at the hospital.'

As the door closed behind him, Alison wondered for a moment what he'd been going to say — what his wish would have been. She sighed.

The situation they'd found themselves in had put them both in an awkward position. But the memory flashes she'd experienced so far were an encouraging sign, and she clung to the belief that it would only be a matter of time before her memory was restored completely and their future was decided.

Alison poured herself a cup of coffee and bit into a slice of dry toast. As she sat at the table, she belatedly remembered the questions she'd wanted to put to Nick, but the moment she'd set eyes on him they'd evaporated from her mind like steam from a kettle.

Perhaps she might find something in her purse, a clue that would tell her more about herself, anything that might shed a little light on the subject. In order to drive Sara to school she needed her driver's license anyway, and Nick had told her she'd find it in her purse in his bedroom.

Excitement soared like a bird through her and, rising from the table, Alison quickly made her way from the kitchen. When she reached the top of the stairs, she turned in the opposite direction from her own and Sara's room. But she'd only taken two steps when a strange sensation shivered down her spine.

Her feet slowed to a halt and she felt as if her lungs had suddenly forgotten how to function. Her breath was trapped in her throat and beads of perspiration broke out on her forehead.

Vague images floated into her mind, but they seemed enshrouded in a fog, making it impossible to distinguish the figures or their faces. She could hear voices, but, like the images, the words were incomprehensible, the sounds swirling around her head before drifting farther and farther away.

'Ally? What are you doing?' The

question from Sara cut through the haze, dispelling the eerie feeling, at least long enough for Alison to gather her scattered wits.

'What? Oh . . . your uncle has gone to the hospital and he told me I'd find my purse in his room,' Alison explained, turning with some relief to greet the child.

'Where did Uncle Nick find it?' Sara asked as she quickly slipped past Alison to open the door to Nick's bedroom.

Alison frowned, following Sara into Nick's room and stopping just inside the door. The room was large and reasonably tidy. A big bay window overlooked the rear of the property, and draperies the color of Wedgwood blue covered the window. The carpet, plush beneath her feet, was a matching blue and the night tables and dresser were made of oak.

A navy bedspread, sporting a geometric pattern, covered the king-size bed, but the bed hadn't been made, the covers pushed to one side. Glancing at the pillow, Alison could see the indentation where Nick's head had rested and a quiver of sensation danced across her nerve endings.

'Here it is!' Sara's voice rang out and Alison dragged her gaze away from the bed to where Sara stood holding a small, black patent-leather clutch purse.

'Thanks, Sara,' Alison said as the child ran toward her. 'What did you mean when you asked where Nick found it?' Alison asked as she took the purse from Sara's outstretched hand.

'You were looking for it before, remember?' Sara said.

'Was I? When?' Alison was at a loss to know what the child was talking about.

'You were packing and you couldn't find it,' Sara told her. 'You sent me downstairs to see if it was there. Don't you remember?'

At Sara's words, a ripple of shock skimmed through Alison. She crouched to Sara's level, sure that she might learn something important — if she asked the right questions.

'That was after your Uncle Nick and I got married, wasn't it?' Alison, managing to keep her tone light, took a calculated guess.

Sara nodded, but it was obvious from the look of anxiety slowly spreading over the child's features that she sensed Alison's tension.

'I remember now,' Alison said in a cheerful tone. Much as she would have liked to question Sara further about that fateful afternoon, she was unwilling to upset the child. 'Let's go downstairs and have breakfast, shall we?'

Sara's face instantly brightened. 'Could you make pancakes?'

Alison smiled. 'I think that could be arranged,' she said. 'Want to help?'

'Okay.'

As they left Nick's bedroom, Alison tucked the clutch purse under her arm, wondering for a moment if she was, in fact, carrying another clue to the mystery.

10

It was while they were eating breakfast that two men from McBride's Garage arrived, one driving a tow truck and the other in a small, white four-door Toyota.

To Alison's astonishment she instantly recognized the car and even remembered that she'd bought it second-hand from a dealership in Seattle. Perhaps she remembered it simply because it was the first car she'd ever owned. Whatever the reason, she felt as if she'd been reunited with an old friend.

As a result she had no qualms about getting behind the wheel, and with the aid of Nick's map they set out for the play-school.

Alison accompanied Sara inside and was greeted warmly by the teacher. Sara scurried off to play with the other children and in the bustle of arrivals

Alison made her escape.

Though she was anxious to look inside the clutch purse, Alison decided to wait until she was away from the school grounds. About halfway back to the house, she pulled into the parking lot of a small shopping mall and brought the car to a halt.

Reaching for the purse on the seat beside her, she looked inside and found a powder compact, a tube of lipstick, several tissues and a brown leather wallet with a change purse.

Flipping open the wallet, she found herself staring at a photograph of herself on her driver's license. The information on the license revealed that she was twenty-four years old and had been born in Portland, Oregon.

Alison quickly inspected the remaining items in the wallet, finding a bank credit card, a library card and a quantity of paper money, as well as some change, in an amount that was neither excessive nor unreasonable.

A feeling of disappointment washed

over her as she sat staring down at the wallet. She had hoped the contents would reveal something new about her, but there appeared to be nothing of any real consequence.

Frustrated, she shook the wallet and to her surprise a small card slid out from an inner pocket. It appeared to be a business card.

Need a Nanny?
Call 555–4343

On the bottom right-hand corner was an address in Seattle, and as Alison stared at the street name another memory dropped into place. She'd trained as a nanny and had been working for the agency for several years.

Here at last was a connection that made sense. The thoughts and questions she'd had concerning the reason for her presence in Nick's house was suddenly clear. She'd come to Bayview to take on the job of Sara's nanny.

But why hadn't Nick just told her she'd worked for him? What difference would it have made if she'd known? She had no doubt, though, that he'd had his reasons. She only wished she knew what they were.

Thoughtfully now, Alison put the car into gear and drove back to the house. Instead of having answers, once again there were only more questions.

★   ★   ★

Nick called to say he'd be later than he'd predicted. And Alison had been in bed almost an hour when she heard his footsteps on the carpeted stairs.

She found herself admiring his obvious dedication to the career he had chosen, but wondered if he wasn't pushing himself too hard.

For the remainder of the week the days fell into a pattern and Alison adapted quickly to the routine. Each morning she would drive Sara to school and in the afternoon they would spend a few hours with Roger. Janet welcomed their arrival and Roger, too, looked forward to their visits.

It was during one of these visits that Alison suddenly remembered that on the day Nick had brought her home from the hospital, when he'd left her alone with Roger for a few minutes, Roger had called her Pamela.

But much as she might have wanted to ask Roger about the woman named Pamela, the opportunity never presented itself as Sara was always with them.

When Alison offered to read to Roger, he chose *The Adventures of Huckleberry Finn*, which, he told her, was a favorite of his. Sara would happily sit on the mat with her crayons and a coloring book, or with the toys she brought along with her.

At times, as Alison read the story aloud, she wondered if Roger was even aware of her presence. He seemed to drift away, often mumbling incoherently about she knew not what.

Nonetheless, she always continued to read, sure that Sara at least was enjoying the tale.

Nick spent the majority of his time at the hospital and while Alison felt a sense of relief at being free of the tension Nick's presence generated in her, she soon had to face up to the realization that she missed him.

Following on the heels of this came the memory of the devastating kiss they'd shared and of the startling need that had exploded to life inside her, sending the blood humming through her veins and a tingling heat skimming across her skin.

But the question of just why she'd been running away on a day that should have been the happiest of her life, hung over their marriage like a dark cloud. And while some of the empty spaces of her past were slowly but steadily returning, there were several pieces, important pieces, that continued to elude her.

It was after dinner on Friday evening

as Alison and Sara, still wearing the ballerina costume she'd worn at school that day, sat in the den watching a video of a Disney cartoon when they heard the front door open.

'It's Uncle Nick,' Sara said as she jumped to her feet and ran from the room, the exploits of Mickey and Minnie Mouse forgotten.

Alison stood up and felt her pulse quicken in anticipation of seeing Nick. When she heard him say to Sara, 'Hello, poppet. Well . . . you look just like a real ballerina. You'd think it was Halloween or something . . . ' The deep rich sound of his voice sent a ripple of awareness chasing down her spine.

'It's Halloween on Sunday,' Sara reminded him.

'But we had our party at school today. Alison said I could wear my costume till bedtime in case you got home. We're watching Mickey Mouse,' she went on. 'Want to watch with us?'

'I'd love to,' Nick assured her. 'Just let me hang up my coat and I'll join you.'

Moments later he appeared in the doorway and, seeing the look of exhaustion on his handsome features, Alison had to fight the urge to run to him. He'd unbuttoned his shirt collar and loosened his tie, which seemed only to enhance his striking looks.

'Hi,' she said, trying with difficulty to ignore the way her heart was drumming a tattoo against her breast.

'How are things on the home front?' Nick asked, and Alison met his questioning glance, a look that asked another question he hadn't voiced — had her memory returned?

'Everything's fine. Nothing new to report,' she replied, and at her words she thought she saw a flicker of relief in the dark depths of his eyes.

He continued to meet her gaze and she felt her face grow hot under the scrutiny. She found herself wishing she'd thought to change out of the jeans and old sweater she'd donned earlier when she and Sara had gone for a walk to collect leaves for a project at school.

'How's everything at the hospital?' she asked, wanting to break the silence that seemed to be suddenly crowding in on them.

'Hectic to say the least,' Nick said with a tired sigh. Turning away, he ran a hand through his black hair, leaving it in disarray.

'Have you eaten? Can I get you something?' she asked, concerned that if he'd been as busy as he'd implied he probably hadn't taken time out to eat properly.

'I must admit, I wouldn't say no to a sandwich, or whatever there happens to be in the fridge,' he said, flashing her a brief but heart-stopping smile.

'I'll see what I can find,' Alison said as she headed for the door. 'Would you like coffee?' she asked.

'A glass of milk . . . but listen, I'll get it,' he hurried on.

'Nonsense,' Alison quickly cut in. 'Sit down, relax,' she instructed, wishing she could somehow ease the lines of strain she could see on his face. 'I know

Sara wants to tell you all about the party at school today. I'll be back in a jiffy.'

In the kitchen, Alison quickly put together a plate of cold chicken, a sliced tomato and leftover brown rice. During the past few days she'd become acquainted with the food store in the small shopping mall and had restocked the refrigerator.

She returned to the den, wondering if, after Nick had finished eating, he would retire to his room before she had a chance to talk to him, to ask a few questions. She'd told him, not in so many words, that she hadn't regained her memory but that wasn't strictly true. She'd remembered quite a lot about her life prior to her arrival in Bayview.

She wanted to talk to him and confirm that he had, in fact, hired her as a nanny. She also wanted to tell him that she was considering making an appointment with Dr. Jacobson as the doctor had suggested.

While it was entirely possible she might never remember what had happened, she wondered if it was too soon to start considering the options open to her — the main one being whether to resume her marriage to Nick.

Carrying the tray she'd set out, Alison made her way back to the den. When she saw Nick sitting on the leather couch next to Sara, his eyes closed, his face in quiet repose, she was tempted for a minute to let him sleep.

'Wake up, Uncle Nick!' Sara nudged her uncle and smiled up at Alison.

'What? Oh . . . I wasn't asleep, I was just resting my eyes,' Nick said with a wink at Alison as she handed him the tray. 'Mmm. This looks great. Thanks.' He set the tray on his lap and began to eat.

Alison sat in the armchair nearby and pretended to watch the screen, though her glance continually flitted to Nick, who appeared to be enjoying the meal she'd prepared.

'That was delicious,' Nick said a few minutes later. 'I'd almost forgotten how good a home-cooked meal could taste.'

Before Alison could reply, Sara squealed and pointed to the screen and second's later Nick's laughter echoed through the room, a warm, enticing sound that set Alison's skin tingling and did strange things to her pulse rate.

Nick lowered the tray to the floor, then relaxed against the leather. Sara shuffled along the couch to lean against him and he put his arm around her. Watching them, Alison felt a glow of happiness tug at her and she smiled, thinking how lucky Sara was to have a man like Nick for an uncle. Alison let her gaze linger on the twosome and she found herself thinking that he would also be a kind, considerate and devoted father.

Suddenly she became aware of Nick's gaze on her and as their glances collided, her breath caught in her throat as a look of desire flashed into his eyes.

An answering shudder of need

sprinted through her and she quickly turned away to stare unseeing at the television, trying to control the ache sweeping through her.

She drew a steadying breath and out of the corner of her eye saw Nick rising from his seat on the couch and bending to pick up the tray of dishes.

'I think I'll pop in and see my father for a few minutes,' he said in a voice that was slightly unsteady.

'You are still going to read me a bedtime story tonight, aren't you, Uncle Nick?' Sara asked.

'I promised, didn't I?' Nick said, reaching over to gently tug Sara's ponytail.

Alison released the breath she'd been holding, wondering for a moment if she'd been dreaming or had simply imagined the look in the depths of Nick's eyes.

Nick dropped a kiss on Sara's head before coming across to where Alison sat in the leather chair. 'There are a few things we need to discuss,' he said evenly. 'Could we talk later?'

Alison swallowed convulsively, affected by his nearness. 'Of course,' she said brightly as her pulse thundered in her ears.

'Good,' Nick said as he continued on toward the door, the tray of dishes in his hand.

Ten minutes later the cartoon show Sara was watching ended and, as the credits began to roll, Sara hopped down from the couch.

Alison stood up and smiled at the tiny figure dressed in a pink leotard with matching netting fluffed out like a ballerina's tutu. Sara looked like a miniature ballerina. As she gamefully tried to pirouette across the carpeted floor, Nick reappeared in the doorway.

'Hey! I didn't know you could dance like that. Well done, Sara!' His voice was laced with amusement.

'Don't I look pretty, Uncle Nick?' Sara asked with the innocence only a child possesses.

'You're absolutely beautiful,' Nick

replied, and as he spoke his eyes flashed to meet Alison's.

The air in the room was suddenly crackling with tension and something more. Every nerve in Alison's body jolted to life and every cell tingled in frenzied response as Nick's eyes bored into hers.

'Catch me, Uncle Nick!' Sara practically shouted, seconds before she launched herself at him.

With reflexes as quick as any jungle animal's, Nick caught Sara in midflight and lifted her into his arms.

'I think it's time this ballerina was in bed,' he said. 'You'll be here when I get back?' He addressed the question to Alison and she could only nod, trying with difficulty to control emotions gone dangerously awry.

She heard Sara giggle as Nick spun her around before heading toward the stairs.

Alison drew a steadying breath, unable to forget the way Nick had brought his eyes to hers. Who had he been referring to when he'd used the word beautiful? Or was she merely reading messages that weren't there?

With a shake of her head, she moved to the VCR and after rewinding the video tape, she turned the machine off and put the tape away.

Restless and edgy in anticipation of Nick's return, she began to pace the room and after only five minutes decided that a cup of tea would help ease the apprehension inside her.

As she waited for the water to boil, Alison tidied a kitchen that was already spotless. She'd grown to love the house, big as it was, and found her thoughts turning to Nick's mother, wondering at the woman's reasons for walking out of a marriage and leaving a husband and children.

She felt a certain empathy for Nick's mother, especially now. Hadn't she tried to do the same thing? But while Alison didn't yet know her reasons for running away from Nick and Sara, she instinctively knew that something traumatic must have taken place that day

. . . something she felt she couldn't deal with.

Unplugging the kettle, she filled the teapot with boiling water and dropped two tea bags into the pot. She was reaching into the cupboard for a cup and saucer when she heard a noise behind her.

The hair on the back of her neck prickled in warning and she knew even before she turned around that Nick had entered the kitchen.

'I made a pot of tea, would you like a cup?' she asked, glancing over her shoulder and trying to keep her tone light.

'Thank you.' Nick's voice, as always, sent a shiver chasing through her, a response she quickly quashed.

Alison took a second cup and saucer from the shelf and carried them to the kitchen table.

'Cream and sugar?' she asked politely.

'Just cream, please.'

'Is Sara asleep?' Alison asked as she crossed to the fridge to retrieve a small jug of cream, aware all the while of Nick watching her every move.

'She should be by now,' he replied, pulling out a chair and sitting down.

Alison set the cream jug on the table and placed the teapot on a small wicker mat used for hot dishes, before taking a seat opposite.

There was a tension simmering in the air between them and Alison did her best to ignore it. After pouring tea into each of the cups she set the teapot aside and lifted her gaze to meet Nick's.

'Why didn't you tell me you'd hired me as a nanny for Sara?' Alison asked, feeling a certain satisfaction at the look of surprise that came into his eyes.

'What else have you remembered?' he asked, his tone cautious, his eyes steady on hers.

'I didn't exactly remember that,' she told him truthfully. 'I found a business card in my wallet and when I read the name I somehow knew . . . '

'I see.' Nick poured a few drops of milk into his cup.

'Is it true?' she persisted.

'Yes, I hired you to look after Sara,' he acknowledged.

'I suppose my living in the house . . . under the same roof . . . is that how our relationship developed?' She felt her face grow hot as she finished the question.

Nick was silent for several long seconds. His eyes held hers in a look she couldn't decipher. The only sound she could hear was the rhythmic drumbeat of her heart as she waited for his answer.

'That's a reasonable assumption,' he said at last, though Alison could see a muscle at his jaw pulsing in time to her own rather erratic heartbeat.

That there was something slightly off kilter was obvious in the tension she could see in his face and in his body, but she had no idea what had caused it.

'How long have I been here, in Bayview?' Alison asked.

'Almost a year. You arrived about a

month after my father's heart attack,' he told her.

'I see,' Alison said. Thoughtfully now, she took a sip of tea. Knowing she'd been hired on almost a year ago helped to explain why her bedroom in particular, and the house in general, felt so familiar.

'Do you remember what happened . . . ?' He stopped and Alison heard the hesitation in his voice.

'No,' she said, and once again a look of relief flitted across his features. 'My memory seems to be coming back in bits and pieces,' she went on. 'A little bit here, a little bit there, almost like putting a jigsaw puzzle together.'

'I admire your courage,' Nick said in a voice that seemed to reach out and gently caress her, temporarily trapping the breath in her lungs and making it almost impossible for her to speak.

'Courage?' she managed to ask.

'Not everyone would have been able to handle all that you've had to deal with this past week,' he said evenly.

'First you wake up in hospital not knowing who or where you are. And when you're told you have a husband and a — let's call Sara a stepchild — you put your own well-being aside and immediately think about the child's.'

'That's not courageous.' She brushed aside his compliment, ignoring the warm glow his words had elicited.

'What else would you call coming home to a house you didn't remember, with a man you didn't know, simply out of concern for a young child?' Nick's tone was edged with anger and yet she had a strong feeling that his anger wasn't directed at her, but at himself.

'Things haven't exactly been a picnic for you, either,' Alison countered. 'You're the one with a wife who doesn't remember you, not to mention a wife who appears to have been running away on the day of your wedding for a reason no one knows. And yet you calmly accept her back into your home . . .'

Alison watched as Nick's expression darkened. 'This is getting us nowhere,' he said, and again there was a hint of frustration in his tone.

'You're right,' Alison agreed. 'Did Sara mention the birthday party tomorrow afternoon at Katie's? It's a sleep-over. But I wasn't sure what arrangements had been made . . . '

'Yes, Sara did remind me about the party,' Nick said with a sigh. 'Actually we told her she could spend the night at Katie's . . . you confirmed that with Katie's mother a few weeks ago, the reason being that it coincided with the masquerade ball and negated the need for us to get a sitter.'

'Oh . . . I see,' Alison said, realizing that she was dealing with a situation that had obviously been planned before her marriage to Nick, before her loss of memory.

She remembered wondering if Nick had suggested they attend the ball in order to provide the opportunity of introducing her, his new wife, to the hospital board members and staff, as well as to the community.

'I said I'd go to the ball on my own,' Nick's voice cut through her thoughts. 'But if Sara's going to be spending the night at Katie's, you'll be here alone. I don't suppose you'd consider coming with me?' he asked tentatively.

The fact that he had asked caught Alison by surprise and she met his gaze, noting his taut features, and noting, too, that he seemed nervous as he waited for her reply.

'Well . . . I suppose . . . ' she began.

'If you'd rather not, I'll understand,' Nick was quick to assure her.

'No . . . I'll come with you . . . I mean, if you're sure that's what you want.' Alison couldn't help thinking that they both sounded so cautious, even shy, like two nervous teenagers trying to arrange their first date — which in some strange way wasn't far from reality.

'You will? That's terrific.' Nick's

enthusiasm was somehow in keeping with her thoughts on teenagers.

'What about costumes?' Alison asked, trying to keep a practical note in her voice while her heart skipped crazily inside her chest at the thought of spending an evening with Nick.

'I believe you already arranged to rent costumes for us, remember?' he responded. 'There's only one place in town that rents them out, and that's Wilson's. I'll stop by tomorrow and find out if they're still holding them.'

'You're not working tomorrow?' Alison asked.

'Only for a couple of hours in the morning. Thankfully, things are slowly getting back to normal at the hospital,' he told her.

'You've been working long hours these past few days, you must be exhausted,' she said, concern for him evident in her voice.

Nick reached over and covered her hand with his, sending a jolt of electricity along her arm and a tingling heat chasing through her.

'You know, you never cease to amaze me,' he said softly. 'You're right, I am tired,' he acknowledged. 'But I want to call the hospital and check up on a couple of patients . . .'

Alison pulled her hand free and pushed back her chair, standing up. 'I'll just put these dishes in the sink,' she said, strangely reluctant to leave. At some point during the past hour, they'd somehow taken a step toward each other, or, at the very least, a step in the right direction.

'I'll take care of them,' Nick said.

Alison hesitated, but only for a moment. She glanced at Nick and was immediately aware that the tension between them had returned.

Perhaps they had taken a step in the right direction, but there was also such a thing as moving too fast, too soon, and she was suddenly afraid that much as she wanted to linger and talk to Nick, if she stayed, she might do something she'd regret.

As this thought flitted across her mind, she quickly made her decision. 'I'll say good night, then,' she said before turning and heading for the door.

11

Alison peeked in on Sara and smiled down at the figure clutching a stuffed rabbit while she slept. Brushing a strand of blond hair from Sara's face, Alison bent to kiss the sleeping child.

She turned and made her way to her own room, recalling once more the unhappy days of her childhood after the death of her parents.

As she undressed and prepared for bed, Alison found herself remembering that the reason she'd pursued a career in child care, and a nanny in particular, had been a direct result of her own negative experiences growing up in the care of her aunt.

Throughout high school, she'd vowed to do whatever she could to bring happiness and love into a child's life on a daily basis. Her first posting as a nanny had been to a couple in

California with two preschool-aged children.

Both parents were involved in their respective careers and Alison's job had been to ensure that the children enjoyed a secure and loving environment during the time their parents were at work. David and Jean Johnston had been warm, loving people who'd spent quality time with their children whenever they could, but by always being available, Alison had fulfilled a need in the children's lives and ultimately in her own.

She'd resigned from her position when David had accepted a job in Australia, and though she'd been sad to say farewell to her two charges, she'd also felt that it was time to move on.

Switching off the light, Alison slid beneath the covers and instantly found her thoughts returning to the conversation she'd had with Nick in the kitchen. She wasn't altogether sure that agreeing to go to the masquerade ball with him was a good idea, but overriding everything was the prospect of spending an evening with him.

That she regarded the outing as a date seemed at first rather ridiculous. After all, Nick was her husband. But the fact that she had no memory of any previous outings — no romantic dinners, or nights at the theater or even a movie — somehow made it impossible for her to look upon the evening in any other light. And as she drifted off to sleep her head was filled with images of Nick.

★ ★ ★

Once again Nick had already left for the hospital by the time Alison and Sara came downstairs. His note explained that he would be back after lunch and in plenty of time to drive Sara to Katie's for the birthday party. He also added a postscript for Alison, telling her cocktails were at six, dinner at seven.

After a breakfast of hot cereal and milk, Alison drove Sara to the nearby shopping mall to pick out a birthday present for Katie. Sara chose a set of kitchen furniture and dishes for Katie's dollhouse and took great pride in finding a card with the number five painted in big bold print on the front.

Back at the house Alison helped Sara wrap the gifts they'd bought, as well as tie red ribbons and matching bows on the parcels. Sara proudly printed her name inside the card and then licked the envelope shut.

A feeling of excitement hovered throughout the house and while it was in part due to Sara's anticipation of Katie's party, Alison silently acknowledged that she, too, was excited about the evening ahead.

Sara insisted on changing into her ballerina costume as soon as she'd finished lunch, and Alison brushed and coiled Sara's long hair into a tidy bun before helping her pack what she would need for her overnight stay.

Dressed in her costume, and impatient now to be on her way to Katie's house, Alison suggested they pay a brief visit to Roger while they waited for Nick to come home.

'He's a little under the weather today,' Janet told her when she answered their knock.

'Can't we go and see Gramps?' Sara asked.

'Don't you look cute,' Janet said as she smiled down at Sara. 'Well . . . just for a few minutes,' she relented, giving Alison a knowing glance.

'We won't stay, I promise,' Alison quickly assured the older woman.

Roger appeared to be asleep when they entered. Sara bounded up to the bed. 'I'm going to Katie's party today and we're going to play games and everything,' Sara proceeded to tell her grandfather.

'What? Oh, hello, missy, it's you. All set for your party are you?' Roger said, then closed his eyes.

'Yep! Katie's mom said we're going to help her make some Halloween cookies, too, and I'm going to stay all night and sleep in Katie's room like I did before,' Sara continued.

This time Roger made no reply and Sara, obviously overexcited about the upcoming party, was having difficulty keeping still.

'Sara, I think we should let your grandfather rest for now,' Alison suggested.

'Okay,' Sara said as she ran toward the bedroom door. 'I'll go and see if Uncle Nick's home yet,' she added, and before Alison could stop her, she'd scampered off.

Alison hesitated for a moment and turned to find Roger staring at her, a faint smile on his craggy features.

'She's a bundle of energy today.' Roger spoke quietly.

'Yes, she is,' Alison replied with an answering smile.

'I was just lying here thinking that Nick is a lucky man to have you. You've done wonders with that child,' Roger said.

Alison didn't know how to respond

to his comment and so she said nothing.

'It's funny how clear some things become when all you have to do each day is stare at the ceiling and think,' Roger continued, the smile lingering on his lips. 'I see now that Pamela would never have made Nick happy. You, my dear, are kind, considerate, and exactly the kind of woman he needs.'

'Pamela?' Alison repeated the name, feeling as if she'd been hit by a speeding truck.

'Nick told you about Pamela, didn't he?' Roger went on, a worried frown creasing his brow.

'Yes, of course he did.' Alison was quick to respond, surprised by the stab of jealousy that shot through her as she spoke, yet fearful that any other answer might upset Roger.

'I'm rather tired today,' Roger said, and closed his eyes once more.

'Then I shall leave you to rest,' Alison said before bending to gently kiss the old man's forehead, all the while trying to deal with the news that a woman named Pamela had at one time been an important person in Nick's life.

Alison slid quietly from the room, her thoughts centered on what Roger had said. He had to have been referring to Pamela Jennings, the odds of there being two women named Pamela seemed remote indeed.

As she made her way down the hallway Alison suddenly remembered that she'd planned to ask Nick about Pamela Jennings, but when he'd asked her if she would go to the ball with him the question had slipped her mind.

She tried to tell herself she was being foolish and that Nick might well have an explanation that would dispel all the questions dancing inside her head. Hadn't Roger just said that Pamela wouldn't have made Nick happy?

'I was just coming to look for you.' Nick's voice startled Alison as she made her way down the hallway, but before she could say anything, Sara appeared at the top of the stairs.

'Ally! Ally! Come and see.' Sara was beckoning to her excitedly, a big smile on her face.

'What is it?' Alison asked.

'Uncle Nick brought your costume,' Sara said. 'Come and show me.'

'Isn't Uncle Nick going to take you over to Katie's now?' Alison asked.

'Yes, but first I want to see your costume,' Sara insisted. 'Please!' she pleaded.

Alison glanced at Nick, who shrugged his shoulders. 'I stopped by Wilson's and they handed me two garment bags. I put one in your room and the other in mine,' he told her. 'I have no idea what the costumes are. You were the one who said you wanted to surprise me,' he added.

'Oh . . . ' Alison said, wondering now what she had chosen for herself and Nick. Would it have some significance? 'It won't take a minute,' she said. 'The presents for Katie are in the kitchen and Sara's overnight bag is . . . '

' . . . by the front door,' Nick finished

250

for her, nodding toward the small case sitting on the floor.

'Please, can I see?' Sara asked once more.

'May I . . . ' Alison automatically corrected as she made her way up the stairs.

'What did you pick? Who are you going to be?' Sara asked before she scooted down the hall and into Alison's bedroom. 'See! Right there on your bed,' Sara added breathlessly.

'I see,' Alison replied, a hint of laughter in her voice, finding it difficult not to get caught up in Sara's excitement.

Picking up the garment bag Nick had placed on the bed, Alison couldn't ignore the ripple of anticipation skimming across her nerve endings. She unzipped the bag and let it fall to the floor and found herself gazing at a stunning peach-colored chiffon and silk dress with long sleeves and a scooped neckline. There were several layers of petticoats under the flowing skirt that reached just below her knees, instantly making Alison think of princesses and fairy tales.

'You're a princess,' Sara announced in a breathless tone, almost as if she'd heard Alison's thoughts and spoken them aloud.

'I think you're right,' Alison responded.

'That dress looks just like the one in your fairy-tale book,' Sara went on. 'I'll show you.' She ran from the room.

Alison held the dress against her body and stood in front of the wall mirror.

'Look, I told you . . . ' Sara came hurrying back into the room carrying Alison's storybook. 'Here . . . ' Sara continued as she placed the book on the bed and opened it to reveal a picture of Sleeping Beauty being awakened by the prince. The dress worn by the princess was uncannily similar to the one Alison was holding in her arms.

The picture on the opposite page also caught her eye. The prince was pulling the princess to her feet, an expression of love and wonder on his handsome features. As Alison stared at the page, a powerful longing tugged at her insides, bringing tears to her eyes.

'Are you going to cry?' Sara's question cut through Alison's wayward thoughts and, glancing down at the child, Alison saw the worried expression on Sara's face.

'No, there's just something in my eye,' Alison said and followed her words with a reassuring smile.

'I wish I could go to your party,' Sara said suddenly.

'I wish you could, too,' Alison responded brightly as she carefully placed the dress on top of the bed. 'But it's a party for adults, and anyway, I bet you'll have much more fun at Katie's.'

'Is the party girl ready to go?' Nick asked as he popped his head around the doorway.

Alison felt her pulse take a giant leap in response to his appearance. It simply wasn't fair that he should be quite so devastatingly attractive. Each time she looked at him her whole body reacted, almost as if he'd physically touched her.

'You're ready, aren't you, Sara?' Alison asked, keeping her eyes on the child and managing with difficulty to ignore the erratic beat of her heart.

Sara nodded. 'You will be here when I get back, won't you?' Sara asked with more than a hint of anxiety in her voice.

Alison felt her heart contract with pain and instantly crouched to Sara's level, taking the child's hands in hers.

'Of course, I'll be here,' Alison said, keeping her tone even. She smiled. 'Now, you don't want to be late for Katie's party do you?' she said teasingly.

Sara smiled, too, then threw her arms around Alison's neck in a hug that almost choked her.

'Come on, poppet. Let's get this show on the road,' Nick said.

Alison kissed Sara lightly. 'Off you go,' she said. 'Have a good time,' she added with a smile.

'I love you,' Sara said before turning and running to Nick.

It was all Alison could do to hold back the tears suddenly flooding her eyes. Blinking them away, she rose to her feet and met Nick's steady gaze, noting the look of gratitude in his eyes, gratitude and something more, something she couldn't easily define.

''Bye!' Alison said as Nick turned and ushered Sara from the room.

Alison sighed as she closed her bedroom door. Sara's declaration of love had touched her deeply and she silently vowed that she would do everything possible to ensure that Sara's small world remained secure.

Crossing to her bathroom, Alison decided to take a leisurely bath in readiness for the ball. She opted to wash her hair first and afterward wrapped a towel around her head before climbing into the scented water.

The warm water worked its magic and slowly she relaxed, finding her thoughts, as always, turning to Nick, wondering if he would balk at having to wear a prince's costume. That must be what she'd chosen for him, she reasoned, and she could only guess that she had to have been in a romantic mood at the time.

She felt a blush tint her cheeks as she tried to imagine herself walking onto the dance floor with Nick, feeling his arms around her, breathing in the rich intoxicating male scent that was his alone.

She shivered in the warm water and silently chastised herself for her fanciful thoughts. But suddenly she was tired; tired of behaving as if she were walking on egg-shells — tired of speculating about the missing pieces of her past.

Tonight she would forget about the mysterious Pamela, forget about why she'd been running from the house, forget about everything, at least for a few hours, and pretend that she and Nick were a happily married couple who were attending a social event together.

Her decision made, Alison felt her spirits rise several notches and as she reached for the bar of soap, her heartbeat quickened in anticipation of the evening ahead.

Determined to look her best, Alison spent some time arranging her hair. After attempting several different styles, she settled on an elegant, yet classically old-fashioned, French roll. Pulling her hair away from her face and off her shoulders, she coaxed the thick swath into a roll, leaving her bangs and two tightly coiled curls on either side of her face.

She darkened her eyelashes with a light coat of mascara and accented her cheekbones with a rich blusher. She even found a lipstick in her makeup bag that was a slightly deeper shade of peach than that of her dress.

When she stepped into the dress and pulled it up over her white lacy camisole and panties, she almost didn't recognize the woman in the mirror staring back at her. Alison felt a fleeting moment of panic. Who was the stranger in the mirror?

A knock on the bedroom door startled her and as she crossed to open it she felt her pulse pick up speed.

'I found two masks — ' Nick began, then abruptly stopped.

They stood staring at each other for what seemed an eternity. Alison's lungs forgot how to function when her gaze skimmed over the white silk blouson, the bloodred waistcoat and hip-hugging black silk pants he wore.

His jet black hair was brushed back from his face, curling just below his ears, defining strong, chiseled features. His eyes seemed to be trying to see inside her soul, glinting like obsidian even as they kept their own secrets.

Their gazes locked and Alison was aware of a tightening in her chest, as well as a dizzying heat sprinting through her. The tension in the air was almost palpable and Alison could feel herself being drawn like a magnet toward him as her body responded to the need she could see in the depth of his eyes.

The sound of the telephone ringing somewhere in the distance filled the silence, effectively shattering the moment.

'I'd better get that,' Nick said in a voice that was slightly unsteady. 'I believe this mask is yours,' he said as he gave her an ornate hand-held, gold velvet mask. 'I'll meet you downstairs in ten minutes,' he added before he turned and hurried down the hallway.

Alison closed the door and leaned against it for several long moments, waiting for her pulse to return to normal. Seeing Nick dressed as a prince had had a startling impact on her senses, leaving her yearning for . . . she knew not what.

It took practically every second of the ten minutes till she felt in control once more. But as she made her way downstairs to retrieve her woolen coat from the closet, she had to tell herself over and over again to relax.

'All set?' Nick asked when he

appeared from the direction of his father's suite. He wore a black topcoat and white silk scarf and Alison could only nod as he crossed to open the front door.

Not without some effort did she ignore the shiver of awareness that rippled through her as she moved past him and out to the Mercedes parked next to her car in the driveway.

The journey downtown was completed in silence and as a result, the tension that had exploded between them outside her bedroom door, slowly but surely returned.

The doorman opened the car door for Alison, and Nick quickly joined her. Together they made their way into the lobby and when Nick's fingers accidentally touched her shoulders as he helped her remove her coat, it was all Alison could do to stifle the gasp that sprang to her lips.

Alison pinned a nervous smile on her face as she watched Nick pull a black velvet mask over his face. She in turn brought her mask to her eyes and side by side they made their way to the ballroom.

The evening for Alison proved to be a mixture of heaven and hell. She was introduced to so many people that after only a few minutes she lost track. Costumes of every description, ranging from the sublime to the ridiculous, from the highly exotic to the simple and most basic, were all in evidence, and Alison found herself smiling at the colorful sights and laughing behind her mask at some of the more outrageous outfits.

Nick introduced her to the hospital board members and their wives and throughout the cocktail hour she was thankful for his presence and his support as he helped her field questions and deal with small talk.

Always at her side, he was like a bodyguard who feared for the life of his charge, but she found that she didn't mind his attentions in the least.

The food looked scrumptious, yet

Alison barely tasted any of it. Seated next to Nick at a table designed to accommodate ten and not twelve, she found his nearness infinitely disturbing, especially when it seemed that their fingers were constantly touching or she felt the pressure of his knee against hers if she did anything more than take a breath.

When the meal was over the orchestra that had assembled on the stage while everyone ate began to play. As the music flowed through the large room a number of eager couples headed for the dance floor.

'Shall we?' Nick leaned over and smiled in invitation, and Alison felt her mouth go dry as she met the challenge in his eyes.

Like the charming prince he so elegantly portrayed, Nick pulled out her chair and bowed as Alison rose to her feet to walk ahead of him and toward the dance floor.

The moment Nick reached for her hand and tugged her into his arms, Alison thought she would faint. Her breath caught in her throat as he waltzed her around the floor and she wasn't entirely sure, during those first breathless moments, that her feet were even touching the ground.

Her chin rested on his shoulder and their bodies seemed to match perfectly, and at every point of contact she could feel a sizzling heat, a heat that electrified her senses, igniting a need she'd never known before.

With every breath she inhaled his rich intoxicating male scent, stirring her senses and sending erotic messages to her brain.

She never wanted the music to end and she clung to him, oblivious of the glances and smiles directed at them as they danced around the room.

When the music stopped it was all Alison could do to stand under her own strength, her head was spinning somewhere in the clouds and her legs felt as weak as a newborn baby's.

'Did I tell you how beautiful you look tonight?' Nick asked in a husky voice, his arm still about her, his gaze intense.

Alison was almost afraid to breathe or to blink, for fear that this was all a dream. Her body was on fire for him and the ache of need sweeping through her made it impossible for her to speak.

'I like the costumes, too, by the way,' Nick went on, humor lacing his tone.

Alison still couldn't find her voice.

'If you keep looking at me like that, I'll have no choice but to kiss you, right here, right now.' Nick had dropped the level of his voice to little more than a whisper, but Alison heard every word and each nerve in her body tingled to life, responding of its own accord to his seductive promise.

When the band began to play, once more Alison felt herself sway toward Nick, the longing to be in his arms again almost more than she could bear.

'Nick . . . Dr. Winger wants a word with you.' The voice belonged to Dr. Jacobson and effectively brought Alison crashing to earth. She turned to see a

Roman emperor wearing a cream-colored toga trimmed with gold and sporting a crown glittering with precious gems.

'Thanks, John,' Nick replied. 'Do me a favor and dance with my wife? I'll be back to claim her as soon as I can, but in the meantime you're the only man here I'd entrust her to.'

John Jacobson laughed. 'It would be my pleasure,' he replied. 'Alison?'

'Fine,' she managed to say, watching helplessly as Nick strode off.

'So tell me. How are you? Has your memory returned?' Dr. Jacobson asked as he drew her into his arms and began to lead her skillfully around the dance floor.

'I've remembered a number of things,' Alison said as she lost sight of Nick in the crowd.

'But there are still a few blanks to fill? Is that what you're saying?' her partner asked.

'Yes,' she confirmed.

'Do you remember the accident, or

the events leading to it?' Dr. Jacobson continued.

'No, I don't remember any of that,' Alison responded. 'But I have remembered most of my past, at least up until I came here to Bayview. Things get fuzzy after that.'

'All in all I'd say you've made remarkable progress in such a short time,' Dr. Jacobson said. 'And that's encouraging. It appears Nick was right.'

'About what?' Alison asked as they completed a turn.

'He was the one who recommended that you be allowed to remember at your own speed, and in your own time,' the doctor replied. 'I agreed, of course, because of the circumstances. I felt confident that, as your husband, Nick knew you better than anyone and only had your best interests at heart.'

'I see,' Alison said, though she wasn't altogether sure that she did. 'I've been thinking about coming in to see you. You did say — '

'Splendid,' the doctor cut in. 'Drop

by anytime,' he told her. 'Oh . . . here comes Nick. He must have done some sweet-talking to get away from Crawford Winger this fast,' he commented. 'Ah, well. I've enjoyed our little chat. Thank you, my dear.' He smiled at her as Nick reappeared beside them.

'I've come to reclaim my princess,' Nick said, flashing a look at Alison that did strange things to her heart.

'Not a moment too soon,' John Jacobson replied. 'I was about to invite your lovely wife to watch the chariot races with me . . . but alas you've returned.' He bowed and kissed Alison's hand before relinquishing her to Nick.

Alison smiled at John, sorry to see him go, but the moment Nick's arms came around her she forgot everything and everyone but the man holding her.

For the remainder of the evening Nick never left her side. It was almost as if he was as unwilling to release her from his arms as she was to leave them. They spoke very little, yet somehow their bodies were in perfect harmony, communicating in a language all their own.

Alison felt more like Cinderella at the ball than Sleeping Beauty, and as midnight struck, she knew this was a night she would never forget.

12

'I had a wonderful time,' Alison said as she settled into the passenger seat of the car.

'I did, too,' Nick said as he made the turn out of the hotel's driveway.

Alison turned her head and gazed at him, instantly feeling the sweet jolt to her senses as she studied his handsome profile in the shadowed darkness of the car's interior.

Throughout the evening he had been attentive, tender, considerate and loving, qualities any woman would hardly dare to hope for, let alone find, in one man.

But Nick Montgomery was no ordinary man. And Alison silently acknowledged that he was the man she loved with all her heart and with all her soul, the man she would love for always.

Tears stung her eyes and her throat closed over with emotion as she savored this moment of self-awareness and rediscovery. For instinctively she sensed that the feelings she had for Nick ran deep and strong and had been a part of her for a very long time.

During the past week, ever since waking up in the hospital and learning that he was her husband, she'd deliberately shied away from thinking about the exact extent of her emotional involvement with Nick.

The fact that she couldn't remember a thing about their relationship, or about anything else for that matter, had been at first frightening and more than a little daunting.

But little by little her feelings for him had nudged their way to the surface, and perhaps the fact that tonight she'd decided not to dwell on the things she couldn't change, not to ponder on the questions she had no answers to, had somehow allowed the emotions trapped inside her to reemerge.

She wasn't foolish enough to believe that with this discovery her problems, or their problems, were over. She knew they still had a bumpy road to travel, but the knowledge that she loved this man, and that her love had weathered the kind of upheaval and turmoil she could only describe as incredibly unusual, was comforting and gave her hope for the future, their future.

'We're home,' Nick's voice cut through her musings and a feeling of warmth stole over her at his words. 'Hey, sleepyhead, open your eyes, or is this where the prince awakens his fair princess with a kiss?'

Though Nick's tone held a teasing quality, she also heard the tension vibrating through it. Alison kept her eyes closed and held her breath wishing, waiting . . . wanting.

His mouth touched hers for a split second of time, just long enough to rekindle the fire he'd lit throughout the evening, then he withdrew, leaving a dull ache tugging at her insides.

Her eyes flew open to discover that he was only inches away, his black eyes burning into hers.

'One kiss is not enough . . . it will never be enough . . . ' His voice was low and husky with emotion and she felt hypnotized by the desire she could see in his eyes. But before she could speak or move, he turned to open the car door.

A rush of cold air skimmed across her face and she almost moaned aloud in despair. Shivering now, she watched him come around the car to open her door.

As they retraced their steps to the house, Alison's heels clicked noisily in the still night air like the ticking of a time bomb as the seconds counted down to zero.

Once inside, Alison came to a halt. Slipping off her coat, she handed it to Nick and stood waiting while he hung hers, then his own.

The tension between them was almost tangible and Alison felt her pulse jump nervously as a handful of butterflies fluttered in her stomach. She didn't want the evening to be over. She didn't want to leave him, never wanted to leave him. But she was at a loss to know just how to tell him, show him.

She swallowed convulsively and took a step toward him. 'Nick . . . I — '

'Alison, please . . . ' he cut in quickly, a nerve pulsing at his jawline, echoing the tension she could see in every line of his body. 'Go upstairs, before I change my mind and do something we may both regret.'

That Nick had opted to make her decision for her was commendable, and she could only love him all the more for wanting to protect her, but in her heart of hearts Alison also knew that her feelings for Nick were far more powerful than anything she'd ever known. He was her husband and tonight she needed him, wanted him as much, if not more, than he needed her.

Terrified that he still might reject her, she summoned every ounce of courage and took a deep breath. 'I love you,' she said with sincerity and conviction.

Nick looked stunned by her declaration and as the silence between them lengthened, Alison's hopes plummeted. But a mere fraction of a second later, the slender thread of his restraint snapped and even as he reached for her, she was already in his arms.

His mouth found hers in a kiss that was electrifying as all the pent-up emotions held in check too long were finally given free rein. When he bent momentarily to scoop her off the floor and into his arms, Alison moaned in glorious surrender.

Breaking the kiss, he crushed her to him and with swift strides carried her up the stairs and into his bedroom. With infinite care he set her on the carpeted floor.

His chest rose and fell as he gazed deep into her eyes with an intensity that sent the blood singing through her veins. His hand came up to stroke her cheek in a touch that was both tender and reverent.

'Am I dreaming?' His voice was a

hoarse whisper of wonder.

Alison smiled and brought her hand up to cover his and press it against her cheek. 'Make love with me,' she said in ardent invitation, and her breath caught sharply in her throat at the desire that flared in his eyes.

Her eyelashes fluttered closed as he brushed his lips in a feather-light caress against first her mouth, her nose and then each eyelid in turn. She felt his hand delve into her hair, gently shaking loose the pins she'd used earlier, until one by one they fell to the floor.

'Beautiful ... so beautiful,' he murmured against her ear as his tongue moistened the delicate skin of her ear-lobe, sending shivers of need spiraling through her.

He found the zipper of her dress and slid it down quickly and easily, until the silk and chiffon floated like a cloud to the floor. With clever fingers he dispensed with her camisole and bra and as his hands cupped each aching, throbbing breast, Alison's legs began to buckle beneath her.

'Nick . . . ' She spoke his name on a plea and he reacted quickly, picking her up to carry her the short distance to the bed.

When he moved away she moaned in protest, her arms reaching out to him. The moonlight shining through the bedroom window was all that lit the room, and Alison held her breath as she watched Nick's silhouetted figure undress.

Though his movements were unhurried, there was still a sense of urgency about them and Alison felt her pulse accelerate as she watched and waited for him to join her. Anticipation had every nerve vibrating with tension until she thought she might snap in two.

When at last he lay beside her, she released the breath she'd been holding and reached out to him as the need to touch became a craving she couldn't resist.

His skin quivered under her tentative but questing fingers and when her hand stroked the muscled curve of his shoulder and continued down his back, he moaned deep in his throat before capturing her lips once more.

As his tongue explored the inner softness of her mouth and entwined with hers in erotic play, Alison whimpered in frustration as the ache in her womb intensified until she was hovering on the brink of ecstasy.

His body brushed against hers, inflaming her senses even more until she was mindless with a need only he could appease. As he carefully positioned himself above her, she was agonizingly aware of the hard lean length of him and she arched her body in passionate surrender.

Slowly, tenderly, lovingly he made her his own, and as a million fireworks exploded in riotous splendor above her, she watched in awe as the stars tumbled down from the sky.

The ache was gone, replaced by a feeling of total and utter fulfillment, the like of which she'd never known before. Nick shifted to lie alongside her and somehow he managed to pull the silk coverlet free and drape it over them.

His arm lay across her breasts, gently possessive, holding her body against his as if he was afraid she might leave. His breath fanned her face and she felt hot tears sting her eyes at the incredible beauty of what they had shared.

A feeling of contentment stole over her, bringing with it a drowsy euphoria, and as she drifted off to sleep, she knew her life would never be the same.

★ ★ ★

Alison let out a sigh as she rolled over. Slowly, languorously, she stretched and opened her eyes. Pushing her hair away from her face, she glanced around the unfamiliar room and her heart missed a beat.

A cool breeze danced across her skin and she sat bolt upright in bed, the silk sheet sliding away to reveal her naked breasts. Her breath caught in her throat as the memory of Nick's lovemaking washed over her, sending a thrill racing through her.

But she was alone. Where was Nick? Her stomach muscles tensed and she pulled the sheet up to her chin as feelings of anxiety and confusion threatened to overwhelm her.

A sound coming from the adjoining bathroom reached her and moments later Nick appeared in the doorway. Dressed in a pair of moss green corded pants and a long-sleeved pale yellow shirt that was still unbuttoned to reveal his smooth, muscled chest, Alison felt a rush of heat sweep over her as their glances collided.

'You're awake. Good.' Nick tucked his shirt into the top of his pants and crossed to the dresser to pull out a tie.

'Is something wrong?' Alison asked, more than a little dismayed by his greeting.

'The hospital called a little while ago. A patient of mine, an elderly lady, and an old friend, is very ill and she's been asking for me,' Nick told her as he deftly knotted his tie.

'I see,' Alison said, silently reminding herself that Nick was a doctor and being called away on an emergency was not an uncommon occurrence. But her heart was crying out for some acknowledgment of what they'd shared the night before — a smile, a touch, a kiss.

'Alison . . . look . . . the timing on this is lousy.' Nick came toward her and sat down on the edge of the bed. Alison tried to ignore the way her pulse accelerated and her skin tingled in anticipation of his touch.

'If you're needed at the hospital, you must go,' she said, keeping her tone light, clinging to the sheet and feeling at a distinct disadvantage.

Nick gently cupped her chin in his hand. At his touch, awareness shot through her like a flash of lightning. 'We need to talk about last night, about where we go from here. There are some things that need to be resolved.' There was a faint huskiness in his voice, a hint of . . . was it regret?

280

Alison said nothing, at a loss to know exactly what was happening or what Nick meant. She had thought that after last night their relationship, their marriage, would be on a brand-new footing, that whatever had happened to send her running away would now be in the past and their lives could go on from here. But with every word Nick spoke, her hopes and dreams seemed to be drifting out of reach.

'There are some things you should know . . . about our relationship . . . ' Nick ran a hand through his hair in a gesture of frustration. 'I realize now I made a mistake, that I should have told you from the start . . . but, I had hoped — ' He broke off and deliberately brought his eyes to meet hers, as though he was searching for something — she knew not what.

'Damn! I'm making a hash of this.' He stood up and swore succinctly under his breath. 'I have to go. I'm sorry. I'll try and explain everything to you when I get back.' He sat down beside her once more and gazed earnestly into her eyes. 'Will you just trust me and believe me when I say that we *will* sort this out?'

Alison could only nod in response. She wanted desperately to believe him, but she'd never seen Nick in a state of such agitation before, nor had he ever been at such a loss for words, and she could only conclude that he regretted what had happened between them last night. A pain the like of which she'd never known before twisted like a knife inside her heart.

The moment Nick was gone, Alison thrust the covers aside and jumped out of his bed. With a sob of despair she gathered the clothes Nick had removed from her with such tenderness the night before and quickly returned to her own room.

Tossing everything onto the bed, she headed for the shower and stood under its spray, trying without success to put some warmth back into her body. She felt chilled to the bone each time she thought of Nick and his love-making, and she was at a loss to know what to do and where to turn.

She let her thoughts drift over the previous evening, to their arrival back at the house. She'd felt sure that Nick had wanted her as much as she'd wanted him.

When she'd told him she loved him he'd looked surprised by her declaration, but she hadn't had time to ponder that because he'd reached for her and lifted her into his arms.

While she silently admitted that he hadn't told her, at least not in so many words, what *his* feelings were, he had shown her quite eloquently that his desire matched hers.

But he hadn't spoken of love. The thought came back to haunt her now. Not even in the throes of passion had he murmured those three words she so yearned to hear.

Fool! she chided herself. She'd been so caught up in her own emotions, in the realization that she loved this man who was her husband, deeply and passionately, that she'd allowed herself to be swept away by the desire that had exploded inside her the moment he'd touched her.

She'd practically thrown herself at him, and she groaned in embarrassment at the wanton way she'd behaved. Shutting off the shower, she stood shivering as tears streamed, unheeded, down her face.

Suddenly Alison was struck by the conviction that the key to everything was still imprisoned in her mind. That if she could somehow unlock the door to her memory, and uncover what had happened on the day she and Nick were married . . . that all of this might make sense.

But how could she accomplish this? she asked herself with a sigh. Maybe if she talked to John Jacobson, if she told him about the memory flashes she'd been experiencing over the past week, as a doctor he might be able to give her some advice on how she could shake loose the memories still eluding her. Surely it was worth a try!

Grabbing the towel from the hand-rail, she quickly dried herself, relieved to have a course of action to follow. She dressed in a black wool skirt and a green silk blouse. Pulling her hair back, she tied it with a ribbon.

Downstairs she located her purse and keys and hurried out to the car. Following the signs through town, she soon found her way to the hospital and after parking the car, she ventured toward the glass doors through which she'd exited scarcely a week ago.

She asked at the information desk for Dr. Jacobson and was given directions to the fourth floor. As she rode up in the elevator, apprehension shimmied through her, but she refused to even entertain the thought that she might be on a wild-goose chase.

'Is Dr. Jacobson in today?' Alison nervously asked the woman seated at the reception desk.

'Yes, he is,' came the reply. 'He's

upstairs at a meeting. May I help you?'

Disappointment tugged at Alison. 'Will he be away from his desk for very long?' she asked.

'Half an hour, possibly longer,' the receptionist replied. 'Do you have an appointment?'

'No. I don't. He suggested I drop in . . . ' Alison wished now she'd had the forethought to call first, but she'd been anxious to take action, to do something.

'You're welcome to wait, of course,' the woman offered. 'Excuse me, but aren't you Mrs. Montgomery?' A tentative smile flitted across her face.

'Yes, I am,' Alison replied.

'I thought I recognized you,' she said. 'Your husband's in his office, at least he was earlier. I just got back from my coffee break,' she added. 'Shall I buzz him and tell him you're here?' She reached for the telephone on her desk.

'Uh . . . thank you. There's no need. I'll surprise him,' Alison said.

The woman's smile widened. 'Good

idea. His office is down the hall to your left and the first door on your right — ' She stopped. 'I'm sorry, I guess you know that already.'

'Yes, thanks again,' Alison said as she moved past the desk and followed the directions she'd been given. She'd never been to Nick's office before, or if she had, she had no memory of it. Though Nick wasn't the man she'd come to see, she could hardly tell the receptionist she didn't want to see her husband.

Perhaps there was a fire exit at the end of the hall and she could slip away unseen. Alison knew she was being cowardly, but she wasn't ready to see Nick . . . at least not yet.

Rounding the corner, Alison found herself in front of a door that stood slightly ajar. She came to a halt and read Nick's name, followed by a string of letters all painted in gold, on the door.

Suddenly the sound of someone crying filled the air and Alison felt her heart lurch as a strange sense of déjà vu washed over her.

Her head began to throb painfully and her breath seemed to be trapped somewhere in her throat. Of its own volition her hand pushed the door open just enough to reveal two figures, a man and a woman trapped in an embrace.

As Alison gazed at the scene before her, the thundering inside her head reached an excruciating level and in that instant the door to her memory was swept away by a tidal wave and the past was revealed at last.

13

Alison stood in stunned silence, staring at Nick and Pamela. Nick's arms were around Pamela Jennings and he was holding her, just the same way he had been holding her the afternoon of his marriage to Alison.

That was the afternoon she'd gone to Nick's bedroom in search of her purse and instead had found her new husband in the arms of another woman.

Alison put her hand over her mouth to stifle the moan of despair threatening to erupt. She took a step back out of their line of vision, thankful for the carpeted floor that kept her presence a secret. Somehow she managed to propel her feet along the empty corridor to the fire exit door.

She drew a ragged breath, fighting the nausea rising up inside her as she tried to cope with the parade of memories tumbling through her mind like a series of old film clips.

As she pushed open the fire door, she wondered for a fleeting second if the action would trigger an alarm, but there was no sudden clanging of bells or wailing of sirens.

The door closed behind her and slowly she lowered herself to the cold cement floor and sat down on the top step. Dropping her face into her hands, she forced herself to take several deep breaths, waiting for the sick feeling to subside, waiting for her heart to stop its frantic pounding.

She remembered! Everything! She remembered that she'd come to Bayview as a nanny for Sara, and had quickly recognized a little of herself as a child in Sara's confused and pain-filled eyes.

With love and attention and understanding, Sara had changed from the shy, withdrawn and unsmiling child into a happy, contented, outgoing individual.

At the outset Alison had found herself strongly attracted to Nick and it hadn't taken her but a few short weeks to realize that not only had she grown to love Sara, she'd fallen head over heels in love with Sara's uncle, her employer.

Nick had been unaware of her feelings for him and she'd kept her secret well. They'd developed a friendship and often, on outings with Sara, were mistaken for a husband and wife with their daughter. Perhaps that had been the reason Nick had come up with the idea of marriage — a marriage of convenience.

When he'd approached Alison and laid out his proposal, she'd experienced a variety of emotions ranging from surprise to overwhelming excitement. But she'd quickly come down to earth. Nick had made no mention of love, and now she found herself recalling a conversation they'd had soon after she'd arrived in Bayview.

He'd told her he had little faith in

love, saying most of the people he had loved in his life had abandoned him one way or another — his mother and his brother. He'd even told her that he'd loved a woman once, but that she, too, had walked out of his life.

Her heart aching for him, Alison quickly realized that Nick's offer of marriage was simply to provide a secure home for Sara. She'd thought long and hard about the decision she'd had to make and in the end she'd accepted Nick's rather unorthodox proposal, convinced that loving him as much as she did would be enough, and that one day he might even grow to love her.

It was Roger Montgomery who'd told Alison about Pamela Jennings and about the fact that Pamela and Nick had at one time been engaged to be married. Pamela had called off the engagement when she was offered a job with a television network on the East Coast. Her career had come first, and she'd gone on to become well-known in the field of television. But according to

Roger, Nick had never gotten over their breakup.

Alison had seen photographs of the inimitable Pamela and she'd watched her on television, wondering how the beautiful redhead could have walked away from a man like Nick.

But now it appeared Pamela had changed her mind. She was back and she wanted Nick. Why else would she have returned to Bayview? What other reason could there be for her to show up at the wedding of the man she'd once been engaged to and throw herself into his arms?

A moan of pain and denial passed between Alison's lips, echoing down the empty stairwell, and she bit down on her bottom lip, cutting off the sound. Hugging her arms around her, she began to rock back and forth, silently praying that the memories pouring into her mind would stop. But the dam had burst and relentlessly the events of the past continued to rush toward her.

The wedding ceremony over, Nick

and Alison had gone upstairs to finish packing for the honeymoon. Unable to find her purse, Alison had sent Sara downstairs to look for it and had gone herself to Nick's bedroom to see if he had brought it upstairs for her.

That was when she'd heard voices coming from his bedroom. The door had been open a crack and Alison had instantly recognized the woman in Nick's arms. Too caught up in what looked to Alison like a lover's embrace, neither had been aware of her presence or of the fact that she'd heard their damning conversation.

'Nick, why didn't you call me sooner?' she'd heard Pamela ask. 'If only I'd known about this I wouldn't have waited so long. It isn't right. I should have come back this summer like I'd planned . . . then maybe none of this would be happening.'

'Pamela, stop it,' Nick had replied. 'What's done is done. We'll just have to deal with it. I did call you, but it's not exactly the kind of news you leave on an answering machine. Please don't cry. We'll work through this.'

Alison hadn't waited to hear more. She'd spun around and run back to her bedroom, reeling from the impact of the scene she'd heard and witnessed. Her marriage to Nick was less than an hour old and already it was over, because the woman he'd once been in love with had returned to reclaim him.

Alison wasn't sure just how long she'd stood in her bedroom as shock waves rendered her dazed and helpless. She remembered feeling as if her world had suddenly been thrown off its axis and she was at a loss to know what to do.

Fearful that Sara would come running upstairs to find her, Alison had tried to think rationally, tried not to let the despair she was feeling override her common sense. Though she'd known from the outset that her marriage to Nick was not to be a real marriage, she had hoped that with time their relationship might develop into a true and loving one. But those foolish dreams had been just that — dreams.

She couldn't recall what had prompted her to leave the house. All she knew was that she'd needed time, time to think through the problem, time to evaluate the situation. Her main objective had been to avoid coming face to face with Nick and Pamela, and Sara, too, for that matter.

The pain she had been experiencing had overwhelmed her and in her rather numbed state, she'd thought a walk might help to clear her mind. Quietly she'd made her way downstairs, sure that at any moment someone would appear and ask her where she was going, or what she was doing.

As luck would have it she met no one. Once outside she thought about using her car, only to remember that it was in the garage for a tune-up.

She'd started to walk down the driveway, with no clear idea where she would go or what she would do. Somewhere nearby she heard a car's engine start and, wondering if Nick was already looking for her, felt her pulse leap in panic. That was when she'd started to run.

All those painful memories and heartbreaking moments had been lost to her when she'd fallen under the wheels of the car and hit her head on the ground. But the sight of Nick and Pamela together in his office had been the catalyst that reopened the door to the past.

Alison drew a steadying breath. She felt as if she had been thrust back into the same nightmare, but this time she was more confused than ever.

For the past week, Nick's conduct had been exemplary and in keeping with the situation they'd found them-selves in. But because of her memory loss, Alison had made assumptions, albeit the wrong assumptions, the main one being that Nick wanted their marriage to work and was waiting for her to give him the green light.

No wonder he'd looked so stunned

last night when she'd told him she loved him! Alison groaned softly in humiliation.

Had he felt sorry for her? Was that the reason he'd made love to her? She felt the blood rush to her cheeks in shame and embarrassment, recalling how she'd thrown herself at him like a besotted fool.

Though she acknowledged that she was inexperienced in sexual matters, she'd believed with all her heart that Nick had wanted her, too. How could he have made love to her with such tenderness, sensitivity and passion when he didn't love her, when Pamela, the woman he did love, was waiting in the wings?

She would have staked her life on the conviction that he wasn't the kind of man who would treat her or any woman with such a total lack of respect. Even after all that had happened, she couldn't bring herself to believe he was a dishonorable man.

What should she do? Running away

was what she'd done a week ago and that had created more problems than it solved. Besides, she'd made a promise to Sara, a promise she intended to keep. And that was another aspect of this whole bizarre mess ... Sara. How could Nick knowingly have put Sara's happiness in jeopardy? It wasn't like him.

Again there were more questions than answers, but this time Alison refused to run. This time she would face the problem, she would face Nick and Pamela.

Taking several deep breaths, she stood up. She wasn't sure how long she'd been sitting in the stairwell giving her memory free rein, but she was cold, both inside and out.

Wondering fleetingly if she'd ever be warm again, she pulled on the door handle and reentered the hallway, slowly retracing her steps.

The door to Nick's office was still open, but this time Alison didn't hesitate. She knocked and went in.

'Oh . . . hello!' Pamela Jennings said as she rose from the chair in front of the desk.

'Hello,' Alison managed to say as she quickly scanned the room looking for Nick. 'I thought Nick . . . ' she began.

'He stepped out for a few minutes,' Pamela told her, then frowned. 'The receptionist said his wife . . . Are you Alison?' she asked.

'Yes,' Alison replied, noting as she did that though Pamela's eyes were red and a bit swollen from crying, she still looked stunningly attractive in a navy suit with a white blouse.

'It's nice to meet you,' Pamela said, her tone friendly as she extended a hand to Alison. 'Nick has told me so much about you.'

Surprise edged with anger danced through Alison and for a moment she was tempted to shun Pamela's overtures, but good manners won out. She clasped the red-head's hand briefly.

'I was just telling Nick that I thought it was high time you and I met,' Pamela continued. 'I wanted a chance to apologize to you in person for monopolizing so much of his time lately . . . I even interrupted your wedding day,' she rambled nervously. 'But I don't know how I would have got through this past week without Nick's friendship and support.'

'I — I'm glad . . . he was able to help,' Alison said, totally mystified by what Pamela had just said.

'Nick and I go back a long way,' Pamela was saying. 'I'm sure he's told you that we were once engaged?'

'Yes,' Alison responded, though Nick himself hadn't told her.

'I know Nick was upset when I broke things off,' Pamela hurried on. 'But believe me, marriage for us would have been nothing short of a disaster. I think we were both a little in love with love rather than with each other. I'm so happy he's found you.'

'Thank you.' Alison was sure she must be dreaming. From what Pamela had said, it didn't appear she had designs on Nick at all. Alison felt her heart skip a beat at this thought. Could it be true? Could she have jumped to the wrong conclusions? Had she in fact been a victim of her own insecurities?

'Alison! There you are.' Nick's voice cut through her wayward thoughts and Alison felt her pulse jolt in alarm when she saw him standing in the doorway. 'Where did you come from?' he went on. 'Lucy told me you were here and I thought you must have got lost, so I went looking for you. Is there something wrong?'

'No . . . ' Alison replied, quickly masking the bewilderment she was feeling.

'Alison and I were just talking about you,' Pamela related with a smile. 'I was telling her how wonderfully supportive you've been this past week,' she added as she stooped to pick her purse up off the chair she'd vacated earlier. 'I must go. I've taken up enough of your time. There's so much I have to arrange.'

Pamela walked toward them, stopping in front of Nick and Alison. 'Thank you for everything, Nick. And thank you, too, Alison, for being so understanding.' She turned to Nick. 'I'll be in touch and I'll see you both at the service?'

'Of course,' Nick replied, and with a wave Pamela was gone.

Alison didn't move, she couldn't. She was still trying to make sense of what had just taken place. Pamela Jennings, the woman Alison believed had come back to Bayview to reclaim Nick, wasn't after Nick at all.

'What brought you here to see me?' Nick's question brought Alison out of her daydream. She met his gaze and felt her heart flutter in response.

'Nick . . . tell me, are you still in love with Pamela?'

A look of astonishment came into his eyes and he stared at her for what seemed an eternity. 'No, I'm not in love with Pamela,' he said at last. 'I don't think I was ever in love with Pamela.

Why on earth are you asking me that?'

Alison ignored his question and asked another of her own. 'Why were you holding her in your arms a little while ago?'

'Because she was upset. I was comforting her,' Nick explained in a puzzled tone. 'The elderly lady I was telling you about was Pamela's mother. Mrs. Jennings died shortly after I got here today.'

'Pamela's mother . . . ?' Alison stumbled over the words, while her brain slowly digested the disturbing information.

'Yes. Elizabeth wasn't overly fond of doctors or hospitals. Though I tried to keep an eye on her, she refused to come in for regular checkups and as a result neglected her health. By the time she did come in to see me, three weeks ago, the disease had progressed too far and there was nothing I or anyone could do. I admitted her to the hospital, made her as comfortable as possible, then I put a call in to Pamela, in Toronto.'

'Is that why Pamela came to the house to see you?' Alison asked as a cold chill began to spread through her.

'Yes . . . that was Saturday afternoon. Wait! Are you trying to tell me you saw Pamela that day? But she was only in the house five minutes. She had a taxi waiting . . . ' Nick went on as he moved to stand in front of Alison. 'You saw her?'

'I was looking for my purse. I came to your bedroom . . . and I thought . . . I mean, it looked . . . ' Alison ground to a halt.

Nick stared at her in amazement. 'Pamela was distraught. She'd just been to see her mother and I was comforting her . . . ' Nick reached out and grabbed Alison by her upper arms, forcing her to look at him. 'Did you think there was something between us? Is that why you ran away?' he asked with an urgency she couldn't ignore.

Alison nodded.

Suddenly a glimmer of comprehension lit the dark depths of his eyes.

'You've remembered. You've got your memory back?' Nick was staring at her intently now.

'Yes, I remember . . . I remember everything,' she said, and a pain clutched at her heart as she spoke the words.

'How? When? Tell me,' Nick insisted.

Alison drew a steadying breath. 'When I came down the corridor to your office a little while ago I heard voices . . . yours and . . . Pamela's.' She swallowed convulsively. 'It was just like the last time . . . you were holding her in your arms . . . '

'And it all came back to you,' Nick finished for her, shaking his head. 'And you thought Pamela and I . . . '

'What was I supposed to think? Our marriage wasn't real, you'd made that clear,' she responded. 'Why didn't you tell me when I woke up after the accident that our marriage was a sham?' Alison suddenly blurted out, anger coming to her rescue now. 'Dr. Jacobson said you were the one who suggested I'd be better off trying to remember things on my own. But letting me believe that our marriage was real was cruel. What kind of game were you playing, Nick? Did you get a kick out of watching me make a complete fool of myself last night?'

Nick held her gaze, an expression of regret and something more simmering in his eyes . . . a vulnerability, a defenselessness there that tugged at her heart.

'You have every right to be angry with me,' Nick said evenly. 'It was cruel of me not to tell you the true status of our marriage, but a desperate man takes desperate measures . . . and I was desperate. I needed time . . . ' he added with quiet sincerity.

'Desperate?' Alison frowned as she repeated the word.

'Yes,' Nick said with a sigh before letting her go. He turned away, and Alison watched as he raked a hand through his hair, an action she found endearing.

'When I saw you lying on the road unconscious, I made a startling discovery. I realized — ' He broke off, emotion suddenly bringing a husky quality to his voice.

'What did you realize?' Alison asked, hardly daring to hope. Scarcely able to breathe, she waited for his answer.

'I realized that the feelings I had for you ran far deeper than mere friendship. I think I went a little insane for a moment, because it struck me then and there that I might lose you, forever.'

He drew a ragged breath before continuing. 'That's when I was forced to face the truth. You see, ever since you came to Bayview I'd been fighting this attraction I felt for you. I kept telling myself that it wasn't happening, that it couldn't be love. I reminded myself daily that loving someone only brought pain and heartache, and I was determined never to let anyone close enough to hurt me again.'

Alison felt tears prick her eyes at the pain she could hear in his voice.

'Nick . . . ' she began, but he immediately put his hand up to stop her.

'Please . . . just hear me out,' he pleaded, and immediately she fell silent.

Nick moved behind his desk and sat down, but the moment he started to speak he was on his feet once more, pacing the room. 'Every day I watched you with Sara, I found myself admiring you, the way, inch by inch, you brought love back into her life and made her whole again. You and that generous heart of yours. You with that immense capacity to love. And with that love you were able to bring Sara out of her shell and help her deal with her sorrow and her pain.

'Every time you made her smile, every time you made her laugh, I wanted you to look at me like that, to care for me like that. I wanted us to be a family and for you to stay with us forever, but I didn't know where or how to begin. That's when I came up with the scheme of a marriage of convenience.

'I kept telling myself I was doing it for Sara, to ensure a loving, secure home for her . . . but I was only fooling myself. And when I finally faced the truth, it was almost too late.

'When you told me you'd lost your memory, I suddenly saw it as a chance . . . my only chance to spend time with you and somehow make you fall in love with me . . . before you remembered.'

Nick stopped in front of her and her heart skidded to a halt as his hands came up to gently frame her face. 'I might regret some of the things I've done these past few days, but there's one thing I'll never regret and that's making love with you last night.

'I need you, Alison. I want you in my life, for always. If you can find it in your heart to forgive me for all the pain I've put you through, I promise I will never knowingly hurt you again.'

Alison was stunned by Nick's admissions, totally bowled over by what she'd heard, but there was no mistaking the anxiety and fear in his voice as well as the plea for understanding.

Alison felt her heart accelerate as a feeling of love surged through her. Was Nick actually trying to tell her he loved her?

'I think I could forgive you anything,' Alison said softly. 'But you haven't told me how you feel about me . . . what you feel. I need to know. Can you say it, Nick? Can you tell me?' she asked, her love for him bubbling into her voice.

A faint smile curved at Nick's sensuous mouth. 'I thought I just did,' he said as he put his arms around her and pulled her close. He gazed adoringly into her eyes and she could see the love, the hope and the promise shimmering in their black depths.

He kissed her tenderly, lovingly . . . and all too briefly. 'What about Sara? Aren't we supposed to be picking her up? We have a lot to do. It's Halloween tonight, isn't it?' he asked innocently.

'Nick!' Alison tried to sound annoyed, but he was much to close and she was much, too much, in love.

He smiled at her, causing her pulse to skip crazily. 'I love you, Alison Montgomery, with all my heart and soul. I want our marriage to be real and I want to spend the rest of my life loving you, only you.'

Alison sighed. 'Would you repeat that please? I've been having problems with my memory lately.'

Nick laughed, a sound that sent a thrill chasing through her.

'Believe me, my love,' he murmured as he teased her with soft kisses. 'I'll never let you forget how much I love you, because I'll remind you each and every day for the rest of our lives.'

'I'd like that,' Alison said moments before his lips claimed hers.

THE END